I SING
OF GRIEF

A Novel of the Trojan War

Michael Fridgen

Paperback ISBN 13: 979-8-9863148-1-5
Hardcover ISBN 13: 979-8-9863148-0-8
Dreamlly Books: Minneapolis, Minnesota

For Myself

CONTENTS

INTRODUCTION

I CAN'T BLAME MY lack of exposure to the *Illiad* on my public-school education, even if I'd like to. I have to admit that I wouldn't have been ready to appreciate the brilliance of the work. Still, it's sad that I missed so many years that I could have spent pondering why Achilles terrorized most of Turkey. It would have been great to attend college parties where the main topic of discussion was whether Helen was hot enough to justify a war. But, like most Americans, my timing was off.

If youth is wasted on the young, then education must account for around 94 percent of that waste. In my perfect world, we'd save any type of liberal education until after mandatory retirement at age fifty-five.

As it was, I managed to graduate from high school, college, and graduate school without learning hardly anything about the *Illiad*. I knew it had something to do with a man named Odysseus and how it took him years to get home because he was captured by a cyclops and some mermaids. And, at some point, there was a wooden horse that people hid inside.

My head exploded when I finally learned that none of these things happen in the *Illiad* itself. Even the famous Trojan Horse isn't mentioned.

THE HISTORY OF THE STORY

When people refer to the *Illiad*, they are usually referencing something called The Epic Cycle. An epic cycle can mean any collection of epic poems that tell a continuous story, but *The* Epic Cycle is always the amazing story of the Trojan War. The Epic Cycle consists of eight epic poems. Unfortunately, only two of the eight poems survive to the present day. We know what was in the others because many ancient Greeks, who actually lived hundreds of years after The Epic Cycle, wrote fan fiction based on them.

Let me explain. Sometime around 1183 BCE, a wealthy city off the eastern shore of the Aegean Sea (in modern Turkey) was destroyed by the ancestors of the modern Greeks. Stories started to make the rounds about what all went on during the destruction of that city, which was soon given the name Illium, or Troy in English. However, Greece did not have a written language at this point (even though the Egyptians had been using one for over a thousand years), and these stories were passed generation to generation orally. Again, it's important to remember that the original stories about the Trojan War were passed along through oral storytellers for hundreds of years.

Around 800 BCE, Greece obtained a way to code and decode their language using symbols—we call this writing. One of the first things to be written down were these amazing stories that people had been telling about the Trojan War. In fact, there are some scholars who believe the early Greeks invented a writing system just so that they could write these specific stories on scrolls.

The Ancient Greece that we know and love, the age of Plato and Socrates, occurs between 500 BCE and 100 BCE. During this time, many writers wrote plays, poems, and stories based on The Epic Cycle. The hundreds of characters in the cycle received backstories, sequels, and lineages. Some of the characters got their own minicycles. Even minor characters were sometimes the subjects of entire spin-off plays. It's sort of like *Star Wars*: there were the original three movies that were expanded into nine, with Han Solo getting his own movie and Baby Yoda becoming an Internet meme. Along the way, backstories and side plots were crafted, like *Rogue One* and *The Book of Boba Fett*. It's actually quite amazing that the power of storytelling works the same now as it did three thousand years ago. (Also, modern superhero movies did not invent the "end-of-credit scene." There is one that concludes the *Odyssey*.)

The eight poems of The Epic Cycle were each quite long. Just the *Illiad* itself takes around twenty-four hours to recite out loud. Of the two poems that survived, we have the *Illiad* and the *Odyssey*. The *Illiad* tells of only a seven-week period during the ninth year of the Trojan War. The *Odyssey* tells of the ten-year journey that Odysseus took to get back to Ithaca after the war. Both of these were believed to have been brilliantly written down by a blind poet named Homer. However, even Greeks in the classical age doubted whether there ever was a Homer. This debate has raged, and even caused loss of friendships, on college campuses to this day. To me, it doesn't matter much whether there was a Homer, or even whether the *Illiad* and the *Odyssey* were written down by the same person. Whoever wrote these poems was standing on the backs of thousands of storytellers who honed the characters over hundreds of years.

The Epic Cycle belongs to us all because we all helped create it.

MANY WRITERS WRITE ABOUT THIS WRITING

Hundreds of authors have written their version of the Trojan War. Each writer gets to choose how they will portray the characters, which plots to include, and where the story will begin and end. You are reading my version of The Epic Cycle—it's the series of events that makes the most sense to me. I also need to admit that I'm selfishly writing this book just for me. I want to have a copy of the *Illiad* that I can use when I get older to remind myself what I like to believe.

When writing about the Trojan War, each author must decide how to handle the gods. In the surviving epic poems, the gods are quite active. Some writers continue this approach, and others ignore them and believe that the gods aren't relatable to modern audiences. I love the gods in this work because they never die. It is, ironically, the gods who teach us about life and death as humans compare themselves to them. However, I do not use the words *god* or *goddess* in my writing. Whoever was the first translator to use *god* to describe the immortal Zeus did all future English readers a great disservice. For us, the word *god* immediately conjures images of the omnipotent being of the Islamic/Judeo/Christian tradition. The Immortals in the *Illiad* are not omnipotent, and their abilities can be limited. Yes, they do live forever and have an impact over their particular sphere of influence, but they are not all-seeing and all-knowing. They are certainly not all-powerful.

THE IMPORTANCE OF THE EPIC

But, why write any of this at all? Why should someone even read these stories? The answer is direct and simple: The Epic Cycle is the single greatest story ever told. While other works of the ancient era are black-and-white with clear villains and heroes, the *Illiad* presents us with complex characters who exist between good and bad. The people of the *Illiad* sometimes make terrible mistakes, they change their minds, they act inconsistently, they surprise, they live, and they die (most of them, anyway).

The *Illiad* is about the meaning of life and the meaning of death. It's from these stories that I learned how to accept my life and my own eventual death. I've received a lot of free therapy from these old Greeks and Trojans. I hope they will do the same for you.

One day, in Greece…

THE BIRTH OF ACHILLES

R*age.* THAT WAS the word King Peleus thought about to describe the foaming seawater on this particular day. The waves of the Aegean Sea crashed with such force against the rocks that they sent huge sprays of water flying through the Phythian air. Peleus wrapped a wolf fur tighter around himself. It had been a warm day when he arrived at the shore, but the weather suddenly turned cold as the wind switched and clouds rolled in from the sea. The water now splashed over the rock on which he was standing, and his sandals were soaked. Even though the frigid water pierced his bare feet, he did not care.

Peleus was king of Phythia. He was in his mid-thirties and stood tall with a muscular frame. His beard was brown with just a few gray areas beginning to show around the edges of his face. He wore no crown.

She wouldn't appreciate a crown at this moment, Peleus thought. *My wife will need to feel that she's in charge of this situation. She may not want to see me at all, especially not in a crown.*

As he waited for his wife, he kept checking the skies for an owl. He did not know if the owl would come for sure, but he highly suspected it.

Nine moons earlier, his wife had suddenly left their palace in the middle of the night. Peleus was distraught with grief and believed that she had decided to leave forever. He spent the next few days weeping in front of the hearth with its blazing fire. Then, one day, an old servant woman came into the room to change the logs. He had never seen her before. She was stooped and walked as slowly as a dog about to take its last breath.

"Don't cry," the old woman said as she approached Peleus that day. "Your wife hasn't left you. She's ill and went into the sea because it's the only place where she will be comfortable."

"How do you know this?" Peleus asked. "She's an Immortal. How can she be sick?"

"While she is, indeed, an Immortal," replied the old woman, "there's one particular sickness that does impact even the greatest among us. Well, at least the greatest women among us. Her sickness will last for just nine moons. On the day of her return, I'll send you a sign. Then, you must go to her cave by the sea and wait for her."

"Who are you?" Peleus asked. "You must be an Immortal yourself to know all of this."

The old woman did not respond but just nodded at him and continued arranging logs in the hearth. When she slowly slunk away and through the door, Peleus was left with the warmest fire he had ever felt.

He waited for each moon to pass. *Thetis, my wife*, he often thought. *Why didn't you tell me before you left? You could have saved me from grief and worry. I had no way to know if you were well. Besides, the child will also be mine. The Immortals aren't known for being involved with the children they bear to mortals.*

Then, after nine moons, the morning arrived that he had waited for. An owl had flown in through his window and perched on the foot of his bed. Since it was an owl that had come, Peleus knew that the old woman must have been Athena. *Owls are hers*, he thought. He immediately got dressed. Since it was a warm day, he was about to leave his chamber without heavy clothing. However, the owl flew into his wardrobe, grabbed a wolf fur with its beak, and flung it on the floor. Peleus obeyed and took the fur.

He ran to the shore and stood there as the weather changed. The owl had not followed him, and he searched the sky for it. Then the old servant woman came climbing over the rocks toward him. He watched as she struggled to slowly reach him. If it had been any other old woman, he would have gone to her to help. However, he did not dare approach Athena as if she needed any sort of assistance from a mortal.

"The time has come," said the old woman when she climbed onto the same rock where he stood. "You must listen carefully to all I say. Have you been inside her sacred cave before?"

"No," Peleus answered.

"Inside, there's a pool. The water in this pool never grows or shrinks. It's sacred water from the River Styx itself and is always there, always in the same amount. She's soothed by it, as all relatives of Poseidon are. You must follow her into the cave. She will insist on giving birth in the pool. It's her nature. But, listen well, Peleus. The infant will easily drown in the sacred water. Once entirely below the surface, the body will be pulled forever downward. You must catch the infant before that can happen. Do not dive in after, or your fate will be the same. You will be tempted,

King Peleus, but do not go into the water. You must save your child."

"Will it be a boy or a girl?"

"A boy. Now, no more questions. Do not forget my words."

She crawled away as slowly as she had arrived. Peleus had been worried the entire morning, but now he was in a panic. Not only had he always wanted a son, but as a king, he needed a son. Badly. He could not allow his son to be pulled into the Underworld before life even had a chance to begin. *Though, it's so difficult to deal with Thetis*, he thought. *We don't understand each other. What if she won't allow me into the cave?*

Just then, as soon as the old woman had crawled out of sight, the weather became even colder. A freezing wind now penetrated Peleus's wolf fur and sent tremendous shivers over his entire body. The waves grew larger. Then, just a little ways from the shore, he saw something moving through the water toward him. Two huge fish, larger than a dolphin but smaller than a whale, swam to him. Each of them had a long horn coming out of its head. Peleus had never seen anything like them before. They pulled a giant tortoise shell that was attached to them with ropes. On the shell sat his wife, curled up in a small ball.

The fish flung the rope onto the seashore, and the shell glided smoothly over the sand. Then the horned fish swam away much faster than they had arrived. Peleus quickly jumped from his rock and ran over the sand.

"Thetis," he said, "I'm here to help."

"Thank you," she replied.

She's favorable to my presence. This is a good sign.

He helped her to her feet. Her pale, white skin shown in stark contrast to her jet-black hair. She was wearing a simple white gown that clung to her body. She was not wearing any jewelry—not even her customary necklace of seashells.

"What kind of fish were those?" Peleus asked. "I've never seen anything like them before."

"I had to go far away," Thetis replied in her melodious voice. "Far to a place where I could be colder. They live in waters that are far from here, waters that are so cold they turn to stone in the winter. They are good friends to have brought me all this way. I pray that Poseidon will help them return to the cold before they get too warm. Now, I must go inside the cave while you wait out here."

"You're too weak," he said. Peleus lifted her with his arms and carried her. She was too heavy for him, but he would not give in to the weight. His son's life depended on it.

Thankfully, she isn't fighting me, he thought.

He took her into the cave and set her on the floor beside the calmest pool of water that he had ever seen. He bent down next to her and peered into the water. There was no reflection, as just a small bit of sunlight permeated the cavern. He could not see any sign that the pool had a bottom. He wanted, badly, to reach into it.

"Do not touch the water," Thetis said. "It's my time."

Thetis placed her feet in the water and scooted herself to sit on the edge of the pool with her knees spread open. She lifted her gown. Without any screams or signs of distress from Thetis, Peleus was shocked to see a tiny head emerging out of his wife. The head went directly under the water.

Gold hair, he realized. *It's happening too fast!*

Peleus saw a small body completely fall clear of Thetis's hips and enter the pool. He acted quickly. In an instant, he shoved his hand through the air and attempted to grab whatever part of the baby he could. He felt himself grab something, but the baby was now completely submerged. Peleus felt the water pulling on his hand. Soon, his entire arm was submerged. Then, he wanted—badly—to fall into the pool with the infant. *I must resist.*

With a giant yell that visibly shook Thetis, Peleus prayed to Athena and drew his arm from the water. He was holding the infant by his right ankle.

"Achilles!" he yelled as he brought the child toward his chest. "You're mine, Achilles!"

Another day, in Troy…

THE BIRTH OF A TROJAN PRINCE

PRIAM STOOD ON top of the tallest tower in all of Troy. It sat in the middle of the palace citadel, which was located on a hill in the center of the ancient metropolis. The sun was hot and relentless, but in its rays Priam could see the entire walled city. *These walls,* Priam thought. *The thickest and tallest in the world. Built by Apollo himself. They will last longer than the great-grandchildren of the baby that is to be born today.*

He had climbed up to the tower to escape the screams of Queen Hecuba, his wife. The screams started early that morning and had gotten worse as the sun rose. *Not to worry. She's given me several sons and several daughters already. Yet, the screams do seem worse this time. I pray that Apollo will spare Hecuba, even at the cost of the child. I couldn't bear to face life without her.*

"King Priam," said a voice behind him. "The priest of Apollo has just arrived. Shall I bring him up to you?"

"No," the king responded as he turned to face the servant. "Let him wait in the great hall until the baby is born. Spare him the cries and pain of the queen. Then, bring him to the birthing room."

The servant left without another word. Priam looked out past the enormous walls of the city. In front of him he saw a large, flat plain that led to a smooth, sandy beach on the Aegean Sea. When he turned his head to the right, he saw the waters of the Hellespont, a narrow channel that connected the merchants of the west to the merchants of the east. On the sparkling blue water he saw dozens of ships traveling in either direction in the Hellespont. Each of these ships had paid for the privilege to sail in the waterway. Priam took his share of all that money. This was how Troy had become the wealthiest city in all the world.

King Priam was not young any longer. He was in his mid-sixties and stood with the beginnings of a hunched back. His long white hair ran in waves down his back, and his beard was just as white. Not a single speck of gray or yellow touched his magnificent white hair. His robe was elaborately made of bright-blue cloth and gold stitching. He wore several gold bracelets. Because he always wanted his children to see him first as a king, he wore the crown of Troy in preparation for the birth.

He turned quickly when he heard loud footsteps running up to the tower. It was the old woman who had served his wife for many years. "Come," she said, "the baby has arrived."

"Boy or girl?" asked Priam as he moved after her.

"Another prince of Troy," said the old woman proudly.

Priam already had several heirs, but he delighted in the fact that it was another boy. *One can never have too many spares*, he thought. *And, princes make great commanders on the field—if we ever need that during this time of peace.*

Upon entering Hecuba's chambers, he saw her stretched out on a bed. She looked like she was about ready to cross the River Styx. He had never seen her in such a bad state after a birth.

"Is she all right?" Priam asked the surrounding women with a concerned expression.

"Oh yes," one of them answered. "Quite fine, actually. She's just tired and needs to sleep. It was the most difficult birth she has had because the infant came out feet first."

"Let me see the prince."

They handed him a small bundle that had been lying on a table off to the side of the bed. Priam unwrapped the tight cloth and held the naked baby up. He thought, *Well, this one is certainly not one to look at. And look at this strange birthmark on his shoulder—it looks like the shape of the Aegean Sea.*

"Don't worry," said the old woman, apparently reading his mind. "Ugly babies always grow up to be the most beautiful people."

"If he does, then praise the Immortals," said Priam. "But if he doesn't grow in beauty, then perhaps he'll be blessed with a great wit. Wrap him tightly. Don't let the queen see the birthmark, she will think it's a bad omen."

Suddenly, a deep voice rang out through the room. "Put that thing down immediately, Your Highness!"

Priam turned with indignation and noticed the priest of Apollo storming into the birthing chamber. His footsteps echoed loudly throughout the room, and Priam was afraid they would wake sleeping Hecuba.

"What's the meaning of this?" Priam demanded. "Explain yourself. And be warned, calling my son a 'thing' is grounds for execution. Even the priest of Apollo must respect the king of Troy."

"I won't apologize, Your Highness, for my feelings are definite. I knew that the queen had given birth even before the servants told me, for the aura of the palace turned instantly dark when the child arrived. I asked Apollo immediately, and his answer was clear. This infant will bring about the destruction of Troy."

"How?" asked Priam. "He's just a child."

"I don't ask questions of the Immortals. But it's a clear message. If you keep this baby, then Troy will be destroyed. You know what you must do. Take it to the slopes of Mount Ida and leave it for the animals and weather to deal with."

"I can't dare even think about that. What would the queen say? We decided moons ago that if this child was a boy, he was to be named Alexander. I won't leave my own blood, my own Alexander, to die in the woods."

"Then Troy is doomed. There's no more to say, as Immortal Apollo has never told me a falsehood."

With that, the priest of Apollo quickly turned and left the palace.

Priam turned to the attendants. "Don't let the queen see the child, even if she wakes and asks for him. Take him to a far part of the palace. Swaddle him and keep him warm until you hear from my servant. I have some thinking to do."

Priam walked slowly out of the room and down a long flight of stone steps. His feet were heavy as he fell deep in thought. *I love all my children. I loved them all as babies. But I'm the king of Troy. Can I kill my own flesh? Can I allow the Trojans to suffer and lose their home? Oh, cursed am I on this day. Apollo, how can you have forsaken me? I've given you all the proper sacrifices and never once forgot my duty to you. Is this how I'm repaid? But the priest of Apollo has spoken, and his word must be true.*

The king walked into the deserted great hall and flung himself onto his gold throne. On either side of him, lining the entire hall toward the doors, were two rows of statues of the Immortals. He was growing bitter as he looked at their unmoving shapes in stone. Then he heard a noise coming from the statue of Apollo. *Oh, forgive me. Don't make things even worse for me.*

But before he had a chance to speak, one of his sons came out from behind the statue. He was waving around a wooden sword. When the prince saw his father on the throne, he immediately ran to him and threw himself on the marble floor in front of him.

"Father," the ten-year-old said, "forgive me. I didn't see you there. I didn't mean to disturb your thoughts."

"You're always a blessing to me, Hector. Get off the floor. You're the future king of Troy, and you should never grovel at anyone's feet, even mine."

Hector was the perfect image of a young crown prince. In fact, he had older brothers, but Priam had named him the future king because he was too perfect to ignore. Everything about him said leader: his look, his manner, his intelligence, and his incredible skill with horses. All this had been revealed while he was still quite young. Priam loved to wonder about the great acts King Hector might one day accomplish.

"What's wrong, Father?" Hector asked. "You look sad."

"I have a great choice to make," Priam replied.

"You told me once that a king's life is a life of choices. Making a choice is nothing new for you."

"But," Priam replied, "this one is the most difficult of my life. I must choose between something I desperately want and something that's good for Troy."

"Oh," said Hector, "then that's easy."

"Easy?"

"Yes, of course. You also told me that a good king must always think of the people of Troy first and his own family second. You said that your own father forgot that once and it led to heartbreak. I don't see that you have a choice. You must think about Troy above anything else—even something that you desperately want."

Priam didn't say anything back to Hector. He stood and slowly walked the length of the great hall and out the door. The sun was blazing hot. As soon as he was outside, a commander in the Trojan army ran toward him.

"Your Highness," the man said. "What do you need?"

"Prepare my chariot and a small guard. Go and get the infant that was just born, the Prince Alexan— I won't say it. Tell the women to wrap him so that I'll never see him again. We'll ride to Mount Ida tonight."

Prince Alexander will be with us, he thought. *But he won't return. May the people of Troy one day know of the sacrifice I made for them.*

Still another day, back in Greece…

THE BIRTH OF A
SPARTAN PRINCESS

Q UEEN LEDA SAT on a stone block in her courtyard. There was some construction happening, and the builders had left a large pile of sand near the block. Leda's eight-year-old daughter, Clytemnestra, played in the sand. Since Sparta was not on the coast, Clytemnestra had not had many chances to play in sand during her childhood.

Leda watched as Clytemnestra put the finishing touches on a rather large sandcastle. Leda was impressed with the detail; it looked surprisingly like the castle they lived in. Clytemnestra then began to construct an army of guards out of lumps of wet sand. She was less successful creating these but was having fun with them nonetheless.

A large wooden door opened on the other side of the courtyard, and Leda's husband, King Tyndareus, walked through. He was her age, mid-twenties, but walked with the limp of a much older man. He had been wounded in a battle just the year before. *Still*, Leda thought, *he walks like a king. I did a good job making him such.*

"I looked for you in your bath, in your dressing chamber, in your jewelry treasury. And where do I find you? In a pile of dirt," King Tyndareus said with a laugh.

"You know our daughter," Leda replied. "Her will is stronger than my desire to stay clean. She loves it out here. She's more active than any boy child I know."

Tyndareus sat next to Leda on the block. Clytemnestra did not give either of them a glance. She continued playing. Tyndareus leaned over, kissed Leda on the cheek, and gave her a warm smile.

It's nice to be loved, Leda thought.

"How dare you!" Clytemnestra shouted at one of the sand guardsmen. "You've betrayed me. For that, you get my foot!" The princess got up and stomped on one of the small piles of sand. It crumbled beneath her sandaled foot.

"Well," said Tyndareus, "that's one way to deal with a betrayer. I don't know if I should be proud or afraid."

"It's probably wise to always be afraid of this one," Leda replied. "She has a mighty spirit."

"Whatever it is, it's not a suitable disposition for winning a husband."

"You don't have to worry about that. She's the throne princess, just as I was. Many men will want to marry Sparta, even if they have to cope with the spirit of Clytemnestra."

Sparta had taken its rules of secession from the Egyptian tradition. Because it was impossible to know who a child's father was, the power of royal blood ran through the females alone. Tyndareus had not become king because he was the eldest son of the previous king. He became king by marrying the eldest daughter of the former queen. It was the queen's blood that was important.

"Regardless of our daughter's harsh disposition," Tyndareus said, "I came to tell you that the contingent from

Ithaca won't be arriving today. There won't be a great dinner tonight. I've already told the servants. You're free to do as you will."

"Thank you for letting me know," said Leda. "I'm a bit disappointed, as I was in the mood for a big affair. But I'll manage anyway."

Leda said this convincingly, but she knew it was a lie. She was ecstatic that the dinner had been cancelled and she now had an entire evening to herself. Because her blood was precious, she had not been allowed to be alone since she began her moon cycles as a young woman. There could never be a chance that she would be impregnated by someone who was not her husband. She was required to have a daughter with Tyndareus to pass on the royal blood. Even after Clytemnestra was born, Leda still was not allowed to be alone in case the child died. But on the princess's eighth birthday, it had been declared that Clytemnestra was strong enough to live a long life. Leda was free. While women in a similar situation may have taken this new freedom to drink wine and sleep with a young soldier, Leda just wanted to take simple walks. And this is what she did, night after night, whenever she did not have to be present at dinner.

She spent the rest of that afternoon looking after Clytemnestra, then passed her off to her servants for a bath. Leda herself also bathed, then dressed in a simple gown without adornments or jewelry.

The sun was setting as she left the palace alone. She walked down through the city of Sparta and an adjoining village. A few people noticed her and bowed, but none bothered her, as they were accustomed to seeing her on these journeys. Tonight, Leda had a lot of extra time. She walked farther than she ever had in the past until she was completely alone.

She came upon a small pond of crystal-clear water that shone with the reds and oranges of the setting sun. There were swans sitting on the pond. Leda sat on the ground next to the water and touched it with her hand. It felt cold and refreshing.

One of the swans was whiter than the others. So white, in fact, it seemed to glow even in the dim light of twilight. *That swan is the most dazzling thing I've ever seen,* Leda thought. *It's more brilliant than any jewel or gold crown in the treasury. How remarkable!*

"He's spectacular, isn't he?" said a voice next to her.

Leda gasped and jumped up with a startled expression. She had not seen or heard anyone approach the pond. She had believed she was completely alone.

"Don't be afraid, I'm not here to hurt you."

She turned and looked at the body that owned the voice. It was some sort of shepherd. He was around her age and height. He was clean shaven with long blond hair that blew perfectly in the breeze. *This is the most handsome man I've ever seen,* she said to herself.

"Who are you?" Leda asked. "And how dare you interrupt the queen of Sparta!" She wanted to assert her dominance and let the stranger know that others would soon come looking for her.

"I care for the one swan," he answered.

"That's it? That's all you do? I've never heard of a swan shepherd before."

"He's a special swan. Please, sit. Let's enjoy the swans together."

"You're not concerned to be caught with the queen of Sparta unchaperoned? You could be killed for this, you know."

"I'm confident that none will find us. I'm even more confident in my ability to escape anyone who would seek to harm either of us. Please, sit."

Leda began to sit, and the man joined her. But as they were lowering themselves to the ground, their hands accidentally touched. Then time stopped moving—literally, time stopped moving.

They sat and talked of life and love. She could not tell if it had been just minutes or entire moons that they had spent sitting next to the pond. She remembered the beautiful swan swimming close to them. She remembered being made love to. She experienced ecstasy that she had never known before. Then, suddenly, time moved again.

The man got to his feet, picked up the swan from the water, and started to walk away.

"Wait," Leda said. "You didn't tell me your name. Who are you?"

"All who have made love to me will recognize me."

When he turned back to face her, his appearance had changed. He was no longer the handsome blond swan shepherd. There was no doubt in Leda's mind that it was Zeus, king of the Immortals, himself. Leda sat and pondered that night for several hours. She was discovered the next morning by the palace guards, still asleep by the pond.

The king had been frantic with worry for the entire night. Leda explained that she had found a pond and was watching the swans when she fell asleep. He rejoiced at her safe return and thanked the Immortals. She made sure to make love with Tyndareus that night so no question about the number of moons would arise.

Nine moons later, Queen Leda of Sparta gave birth to a daughter. She was the most beautiful baby anyone in the palace had ever seen. Only Leda knew that the baby had received her beauty from her true father, Zeus.

"What shall we name her?" Tyndareus asked.

"Helen," Leda answered. "Helen of Sparta."

Twelve years later…

ACHILLES MEETS HIS MATCH

THE BRILLIANT SPARKLE of his own golden hair sometimes flashed past his eyes as twelve-year-old Achilles jumped from a wooden structure right outside the Phythia Palace. He was attempting to complete the course in record time, but he also wanted to impress the trainer watching him with his strength. He came to the next obstacle. Quickly and seemingly without effort, Achilles grabbed a spear from the ground and threw it at a wooden target. It hit directly in the center and shattered the entire piece of wood. He laughed.

He ran fast toward the finish line and stared directly into the eyes of the trainer. He wanted the man to feel fear at his speed. However, King Peleus's dog, a small pup named Little Heracles, came prancing and settled right in front of the finish line. Achilles grunted a little and kicked the dog to the side. The pup ran and cowered next to a flagpole, whining with slight pain.

"How was that?" Achilles asked. "It was the fastest, right? I could feel it."

"Very fast," the trainer answered. "The fastest yet. But what would Chiron say about how you kicked that dog?"

Achilles grimaced inside. As much as he respected Chiron, the mighty teacher of warriors, he did not like being reminded to always live up to his ideals.

"Chiron doesn't always understand. With him it's all about efficiency and choices. I'm sick of it. No soldier on the battlefield is ever going to let a dog get in the way of victory."

"But we aren't on a battlefield right now. When do you go back to Chiron, anyway?"

"Next moon. And don't go and tell him about the dog. He'll harp on it for weeks and won't let any training get done until he feels I've become remorseful enough."

"I'll leave now," the trainer said, looking in the distance. "Your father is coming from the palace and my time is done."

The trainer turned and walked away from the palace. Achilles ran back over to another wooden structure and, with a single leap, perched himself on top of it. His golden hair flying in the wind made his dirty everyday armor look even more rough than it already was. Similarly, the dirt on his face made his eyes look more like the Aegean Sea than they normally appeared.

Achilles noticed his father walking toward the training field. But, suddenly, his eyes were drawn to someone walking slightly behind the king. It was a boy, perhaps just a year or so older than himself. He was dressed in fine clean clothes. *His hair is almost as black as Mother's*, Achilles thought. *His eyebrows are also as dark, and so perfectly shaped.* Somehow, Achilles knew that the last person he would think about before he died would be this boy. *What a strange thought to have! I should learn his name.*

King Peleus looked around for Achilles. The clean boy also looked around then noticed Little Heracles whimpering next to the flagpole. He walked up to the dog, bent down, and stroked his fur. Then the boy picked up the pup and played with him in his arms.

"Achilles!" Peleus shouted when he noticed him. "Come down from there. There's someone I want you to meet."

Achilles jumped down from his perch as swiftly as he'd mounted it. He hoped the boy noticed, but he'd been looking at the dog instead.

"Achilles, meet Patroclus," Peleus said. "He's the son of Menoetius."

"The Argonaut?" Achilles asked.

"Yes, of course," his father replied. "He's going to stay with us for many moons. He'll accompany you to stay with Chiron for the winter. Make him welcome. You should think of him like a brother and treat him as such. Menoetius is a good friend of mine and I'm happy to do him this favor."

With that, King Peleus retreated toward the palace. Achilles grabbed a spear from the ground and used it to lean on. Patroclus noticed him and walked toward him. When he was close, Little Heracles jumped from his arms and ran away.

"Little Heracles must like you," Achilles said. "He never lets me hold him."

"Who?" Patroclus asked.

"The dog. He's Little Heracles."

"Oh, he's a sweet little thing."

"I'm Achilles."

"I know. I've heard about your gold hair and your Aegean eyes. I now see that it's all true."

"What did you do to get sent here?" Achilles asked abruptly. "Must have been something really terrible."

"How do you know I did something?" Patroclus replied.

"Because it doesn't make sense that you're just coming here to live with us. Why leave your own father? Plus, you're going to accompany me to live with Chiron. Chiron doesn't waste his time on anyone who doesn't need to learn something."

"Well, yes," said Patroclus, "I did do something. They don't think I know what I did—my father and the others. They're trying to spare my feelings, but I overheard them talking. I killed another boy."

"How does someone kill someone else and not know it? My mother says that I was born to kill, and I've never killed anyone. But I think that if I did, I would surely remember."

"Is your mother really an Immortal who lives by the sea?"

"Yes."

"Do you visit her? Does she talk like us?"

"I visit her often and, of course, she talks just like us. How else would we speak to each other? I'll take you to see her. But, don't change the subject. How does someone kill someone else and not know about it?"

"I was playing a game with this other boy about my age. Hounds and Jackals. It's an Egyptian game. Do you know it?"

"Of course," Achilles answered, "Chiron love that game of strategy. We play often."

"Well," Patroclus continued, "we were playing and he was cheating. I just got so mad that I pushed him. His chair fell backward and he hit his head. They took him away. I didn't know he died until I overheard my father talking about it. My father thinks that I have the best heart ever born in Greece, and he doesn't want me to be stained by the act of violence. So he sent me here to learn from Chiron."

"What did it feel like to kill someone?" Achilles asked.

"I didn't feel anything at the time, but after I found out that he died, I got sad and cried. I cried a lot, actually."

"Why? The boy was cheating. Doesn't any part of you feel good that he got what was coming to him? The Immortals must have willed this to happen."

This kid Patroclus is strange to admit crying to another boy, Achilles thought. *I would never admit to crying in front of anyone, let alone a complete stranger. He must really have a different heart from other Greek men.*

"I didn't cry for the boy," said Patroclus. "I cried for his parents because I knew they would miss him. And, I guess, I cried for myself because I didn't want to get in trouble or have to leave."

"Don't worry. I'll make sure that you're welcome here. And you'll love Chiron—because I can tell already that he's really going to like you. He likes people who have a heart. Sometimes I think that he hates me. It's complicated, but you'll soon see. Just stick with me, Patroclus, and I'll make sure that you never cry again."

One moon later...

ACHILLES AND PATROCLUS ON MOUNT PELION

THEY WERE ON their way to join Chiron. Patroclus tried as hard as he could to keep up with Achilles. During the past moon, he had gotten used to walking quickly in order to be anywhere near his new friend. But now, as they were climbing Mount Pelion, Patroclus found it nearly impossible to keep Achilles within sight.

"Could you keep us mere mortals in mind?" Patroclus shouted ahead.

"I am mortal!" Achilles shouted back.

"Sort of, I guess," Patroclus said to himself.

He watched as Achilles walked even faster then sprinted toward a rock. He did a summersault in the air, briefly landed on the rock, and summersaulted off it again. He landed in a bush and pushed through it.

I'll just walk around the rock, Patroclus thought. But as Patroclus stepped around it, he noticed that Achilles was limping a bit up ahead. He had never seen even the slightest sign of pain in him before. *Maybe he's as mortal as me.* Then he ran to catch up. "Achilles, did you hurt yourself?" he asked.

"Me? No, it's just a scratch or something. Let's keep on going."

"Stop and let me look at it."

Achilles stopped and sat on another large rock. Patroclus knelt and placed Achilles's sandaled foot in his lap. A large thorn was lodged in his right heel. It had ripped a sizable tear through the skin. Patroclus yanked out the thorn without telling Achilles about it.

"What did you just do?" Achilles shouted as loud as Patroclus had ever heard him shout. "That hurt!"

"I pulled out a big thorn," Patroclus replied. "You have a pretty big gash from it."

Patroclus retrieved the waterskin that was hanging around his back. He used it to wash the wound. Then he ripped a strip of fabric off the bottom of his tunic and tied it tightly around Achilles's ankle. "You have to keep this clean," he said.

"Why?" Achilles asked. "Dirt never hurt anyone. I practically live in it."

"While you've been running around jumping over everything in your way, I've been spending my life observing things. I've seen lots of wounds. Trust me—keep it clean, or it will fester and you'll die."

"Unlikely, but whatever you say."

Patroclus gathered his things and started walking again. This time, Achilles kept right at his side at a normal walking pace.

"I think the words you're looking for," said Patroclus, "are thank you."

"What? Oh yes, thank you, Patroclus. You've saved my life."

"That better not be sarcasm."

"It was, but I'm sorry. My mother told me to be nice to you."

"Thetis knows who I am?"

"Of course. I talk about you all the time. She thinks you're good for me, thinks I could use your influence. She told me that no matter what I do during the day, no matter what kind of battle I'm fighting, I must always focus on spending the evening with you. I think it's her way of telling me that I better not get myself killed."

Patroclus was glad to hear the words of Thetis. They filled him with great joy, and he smiled at Achilles. Achilles smiled back.

It had become cold and damp as they climbed high enough on Pelion to encounter a strong breeze coming from the top of the mountain. When they'd begun the journey, Patroclus was dismayed at having to carry so much fur in this pack, but now he was happy that he had. He knew he'd be spending the winter in a cave and hoped he'd survive reasonably intact.

"There's Chiron now," Achilles said and pointed up ahead to a large outcropping of rock.

Patroclus saw a man with long brown hair and a shirtless, muscular body. He was clean shaven and sitting on a large gray horse.

"I've never seen a horse that still before," said Patroclus. "And that large."

"That's because it's not a real horse," Achilles replied. "It's a large rock that Heracles carved into a horse when he was training up here. Chiron loves it and sits on it all the time. He's practically attached to it."

"Heracles himself was here?"

"Yes, but don't ask Chiron about it. He doesn't like to tell one student about another. He's weird, but you'll get used to it."

Suddenly, Chiron stood on top of the sculpture and swung a huge axe in the air around his neck. He threw it fiercely in the direction of the boys. Patroclus gave a small shout of alarm and ran off the side of the path. Achilles, calm as ever, just reached one hand up and grabbed the axe as it came rotating toward him through the air.

"Don't worry," said Achilles. "That's his way of telling me to go and get firewood. He wants to talk to you alone. Take my pack. Patroclus. He'd never hurt either one of us."

Achilles gave his pack to Patroclus and then ran off into the forest. Patroclus struggled with the extra burden, but he managed to get up to the opening of the cave.

Chiron jumped off the horse sculpture. "You must be Patroclus, the healer," he said.

His voice is deep, thought Patroclus. *And I think it's full of love, maybe? Maybe not? But, I'm not a healer.* "I'm Patroclus, but I'm not a healer," he replied.

"You patched up Achilles with skill."

"How do you know?"

"Nothing happens on Mount Pelion that I don't know about. I've lived here for so long that I've become part of the mountain, I think. I don't even feel the cold anymore. But I sent Achilles to get firewood so that the two of you stay warm. Come inside."

Patroclus followed him into the cave. It was much larger than he had expected. Surprisingly, two proper beds were placed near one of the sides and next to a natural hearth.

"I sleep outside," Chiron said. "Put your things by the beds. Why are you here, Patroclus?"

Patroclus dumped their stuff on the rock floor and sat on the bed. "I killed another boy, I guess. I didn't mean to, but it happened because I got mad. I'm here to atone and learn to fight like Achilles."

"That's incorrect. You don't need to atone. Atone means to deal with an unpleasant emotion and move on from it. You should never move on. You must always remember what it feels like to kill. Your heart is your asset. Don't let it stop feeling. And you're not a fighter like Achilles. You never will be."

"Then why am I here?"

"Just like all the others, you're here to learn from me. Together we'll practice using herbs to make poultices. We'll perfect the art of keeping wounds clean. I'll show you how to help a man not be in so much pain."

They heard a loud thud at the entrance to the cave. Achilles stood next to an enormous pile of logs, enough for at least a moon.

"All done," Achilles said. "And in record time!"

Chiron rolled his eyes at Patroclus.

I think I'll really like it here with Chiron, Patroclus thought.

.

A few years later, back in Troy…

PARIS THE SHEPHERD

TWELVE SHEEP WERE scattered about a small meadow on the side of Mount Ida. The shepherd boy, Paris, sat on the grass among them. He was high enough on the mountain that he could see the towers of Troy far away in the distance, just before the long blue line of the sea. *The towers of Troy are magnificent,* Paris thought. *I wonder what it would be like to live in such a place.*

This may very well have been the day of his birth, but Paris had no way of really knowing that. Sixteen years earlier, on this day, his parents found him lying in the grass at this very spot. They were simple farmers who had prayed to the Immortals for a child. They named him Paris. They never hid the fact from him that he wasn't their natural child, but they always loved him as if he were.

He liked this spot because it reminded him of his parents, who were now across the River Styx. He also liked its seclusion. Ever since he'd become a man, girls from the lower village had been climbing up to watch him with the sheep. At first he was uncomfortable with how they gawked at him. He thought that he must be disfigured in some way. But then he learned that they wanted to see him because, as one girl put it, he was a man from the most beautiful dream a woman could ever have. That was when he realized he was quite good-looking. It was fun at first, playing around with them. Still, on days like today, he needed a break from all of that. *I've lost too many sheep during all that frolicking about, anyway,* he thought. *Now that I'm on my own, I need to be more careful or I'll starve. I can't live on frolicking alone. But it sure would be a nice life.*

The weather had been dreary that morning. Now it had cleared up to become the most beautiful day Paris could remember. The temperature was perfect for being outside and away from the cabin he'd shared with his adopted parents before they died.

One of the sheep, a small runty one, suddenly decided to run away from the meadow and headed toward the side of the mountain. It surprised Paris, as this sheep was usually the slowest of them all. Since the herd was content eating in the meadow, Paris got up and followed the runt.

Along the sheer rock side of the mountain, the sheep came to a stop in front of a large crack. *I've grown up in this place and never noticed that crack before,* Paris thought. *It must be new. But there's light coming from it.*

"Hello?" Paris called into the cave. "It's a shepherd. Is anyone in there?"

The crack remained silent. *Someone must be in there. How else could there be light? Is this a cave?*

Paris squeezed between the jagged rocks and entered the crack. He gasped out loud when he saw the inside.

It was a cave in the sense that it was a room made of rock, but the rock was completely smooth on all four sides, just as the ceiling and floor were. He looked for the fire that made the light but couldn't find it. The light was coming from the walls of the cave itself. Then he gasped again when he saw three women standing against the far wall.

"Come close, Paris," said one of them. "We've been expecting you."

He walked toward them. They were of equal height, and Paris knew that they must be Immortals. *No mortal women could shimmer like these.* One had long shining brown hair in braids, one had blond hair tied up on top of her head, and the third had cascading curls of red perfectly flowing down her back. They each wore a white tunic and was adorned with various types of gold jewelry.

"Paris," said the one in brown braids. "You're not the strongest man in the world. You're not the most masculine. However, you are, Paris, the most beautiful man who has ever walked the Earth. The Immortals admire your beauty. The three of us even fight about it. It has been a long time—"

"We've brought you here for a task," interrupted the blond.

Paris now heard something behind him. He turned, startled, and saw the runty sheep coming toward him. The sheep had an object in its mouth. Paris bent down and retrieved it—an apple made entirely of solid gold. *How did the runt manage to carry this? And where did it come from?* he wondered.

"You must choose," said the braided woman. "Choose which of us is the most beautiful. We have long fought over it, and now it is you who will decide. Give the apple to the one you choose."

"Choose me, Paris," said the blond. "I'm Hera. I'm the Immortal spirit of family and home. If you choose me, you'll live a long and very happy life surrounded by your children and grandchildren. Your toils will be easy, and you'll have an agreeable wife you'll love to talk to."

"Choose me, Paris," said the woman in brown braids. "I'm Athena, the Immortal spirit of wisdom. Choose me, and you'll become wise among men. You'll be respected and sought out for your knowledge. You'll feel pride that others seek your counsel."

The third woman had so far been silent. Paris looked to her, and she raised one eyebrow. She sat herself down, right on the floor, and arranged her clothing around her. She rubbed her golden necklace delicately as she spoke.

"Paris," she said, "I'm Aphrodite, the Immortal spirit of love. If you give me my rightful place as the most beautiful of the Immortals, I'll grant you the most beautiful woman in the world. You'll have a great love affair, with passion that no mortal has ever experienced before. You'll be the envy of all men who desire what you have."

Paris rubbed the shiny apple in his hand. *Is there even a choice?* he asked himself. *The Immortals like to trick us humans, but the choice in this matter seems clear. I can always learn on my own and grow in wisdom. I can always have children and a family. But to get a passionate woman who is also the most beautiful? Now, that's the best way to get whatever else I want.*

He walked slowly over the rock floor and handed the apple to Aphrodite. When she took it, a low rumbling was heard coming from the outside. Suddenly, the other two women vanished. Aphrodite stood and smiled at him.

"You've chosen well," she said. "Now, I'll set you on your way. You'll keep your name, Paris, for that will honor those who saved you from an infant death. But know that it isn't your birth name."

"I know," Paris said. "I was born and discarded. Paris is the only name—"

"Be quiet and listen. You were born Alexander, the prince of Troy, son of King Priam and Queen Hecuba, brother to the mighty Hector. Your place isn't here among the sheep and the silly village girls I've allowed you to sleep with. From now on, you're a prince, and you'll save yourself for your one true love, the most beautiful woman in the world."

"Where will I find her? What am I to do?" he asked her. But he thought, *I should go to Troy. But will they believe me? I'm a prince!*

"I'll set you on your course. You'll leave this place, leave all the sheep behind. Go to Troy. I'll see that you're easily admitted to an audience with the king. There, show him your birthmark of the Aegean Sea. Tell him how you were saved. I promise you, Paris, tonight you'll sleep in the finest bed with the finest linens of Troy."

AGAMEMNON CHOOSES A BRIDE

"WAKE UP, CLYTEMNESTRA," said a servant woman. "You've slept too long, and it's time to prepare. King Agamemnon is already here."

Clytemnestra grunted and rolled over in her bed. She opened her eyes slightly and saw the morning light coming through the window. "It's morning," she said. "Why can't all this wait until later? Shouldn't we wait for a dinner or something more formal? What's to be done in the morning?"

"A whole day has been planned, my lady. The king and queen have ordered that all of Sparta line the streets as King Agamemnon passes."

"He's just another king—same as father. Why all the bother?"

"Agamemnon is king of Mycenae, the most important and powerful kingdom in all of Greece. The king and queen of Sparta are right to do well by him. And, he's to be their son-in-law."

"Ugh! Helen!" Clytemnestra grunted loudly. *Always Helen,* she thought. *My life has revolved around that beautiful face since the day it was born. How cursed am*

I to have a younger sister who outshines me in every way!
Except in shrewdness and intelligence. Those belong to me.

"I think I'll just stay in bed," Clytemnestra said. "Everyone knows that Agamemnon is here to wed Helen. I'll just spoil all the fun."

"It's your parents' orders."

Clytemnestra grunted one last time and finally crawled out of bed. During her dressing, she fought bitterly with her servants. They wanted to adorn her with gold and paint her face. But, as usual, Clytemnestra was the victor as she left the room in a red gown without adornments and paint. She knew her mother would not be pleased if she noticed her, but with Helen in the room, it was unlikely anyone would notice her.

She descended a stone staircase and entered the great hall. Everything was in place for the royal family to receive their guest. The king and queen were already sitting on their grand thrones. Neither of them looked at her when she walked in and took her rightful place next to her father. She sighed.

It seemed to take forever for Helen to arrive. She finally glided into the room. Everyone, all the servants, stopped to stare at her. *Yes, she's beautiful,* Clytemnestra thought. *Get over it. She has the same face that she always has.*

Helen bowed to her family and took her place next to her mother.

Soon, all the servants backed up against the stone walls as the giant doors to the hall opened. Without fanfare, King Agamemnon strolled into the room with just an entourage of one servant man. Clytemnestra was surprised by this. She had expected the exalted monarch to descend from on high. *He looks like a soldier,* she mused. *A rough soldier who has seen several battles already. Not very smart,*

I think, but extremely daring. He would make a fun hus-
band. He'll be wasted on Helen.

Her father, King Tyndareus, stood and said, "Welcome, King Agamemnon of Mycenae. The people of Sparta welcome you as their own."

"And greetings to you," Agamemnon replied. "All of Mycenae is eager for me to return with their new queen."

"It's true what they say, you don't waste time," Tyndareus said.

"I pride myself on my ability to make decisions quickly. Sometimes too quickly, my aides tell me. But I believe that indecision gives the enemy an advantage. So yes, I come to take your daughter for a bride and bring back a queen for Mycenae. My people have been without a queen since I took the throne."

"Then," said Tyndareus, "let us drink to you and Helen. May you live long and in peace."

Clytemnestra noticed a sudden and scornful look cross Agamemnon's face. He looked both confused and annoyed at the same time.

"I do hope to live long," Agamemnon said, "but never in peace. However, Tyndareus, there must be a mistake. Did you meet with my chancellor this morning? He was to have arrived before me to settle all this."

"I've met with nobody," King Tyndareus replied. "No one arrived from Mycenae before you."

"Well, that explains it. I'm afraid this is a bit awkward. Perhaps we should go and speak alone, Tyndareus."

Tyndareus motioned, and Agamemnon followed him into the private receiving chamber. The women stood and bowed as he passed.

What's this all about? Clytemnestra wondered. *I su-*
ppose Agamemnon wants both Helen and the throne of

Sparta. Well, I'm the throne princess, and he'll have to reckon with me. And if Father thinks that he can—

"Clytemnestra," said the queen. "Did you just climb out of bed? Your face isn't even painted! Girl! One of these days I'll pray that the Immortals teach you a proper lesson."

"Don't get all upset, Mother," Clytemnestra replied. "Helen is as beautiful as ever. She comes with beauty, and I come with the throne. Shouldn't that be enough for me? Why bother with all the paint and gold?"

The queen said, "I just don't understand—"

She was interrupted by the two kings returning. They were both laughing loudly as they entered. They had their arms around one another.

Now what's this all about? Clytemnestra asked herself. *And why is Agamemnon staring at me? Is he already plotting to have his wife's sister, me, killed? Then he can have Helen and the throne.*

"There has been a great misunderstanding," King Tyndareus began as he stood next to Queen Leda. "Yes, King Agamemnon has heard of Helen's great beauty and came to honor our family."

"And everything I heard is true," Agamemnon said.

Of course it is, Clytemnestra thought.

"But," Tyndareus continued, "he's also heard of Clytemnestra's strong constitution and ability to make decisions without a second thought. Clytemnestra, you'll marry Agamemnon and become the queen of Mycenae. Helen, you're now the throne princess of Sparta."

Clytemnestra was stunned. *Oh!* she thought. *I really should have put on at least some gold.*

A few years after Agamemnon
married Clytemnestra…

ACHILLES FORMS AN ARMY

A CHILLES KICKED A man in the head to make sure he was really dead. When the man didn't move any longer, Achilles stood straight and surveyed the battlefield. Just a few men were still scrapping with each other, and all of the actual fighting was done. He'd joined Agamemnon for the war and was glad when he saw the flag of Mycenae flying from the castle of Locrist. They had won.

Since all the fighting was over, Achilles starting walking across the field to his tent. He stopped to position his sword back through his belt and check that his armor was intact. His parents had presented him with the armor on his seventeenth birthday, and he cherished it. *It's dirty and has blood on it, but it will clean up as it always does*, he thought as he continued walking.

He stepped over the occasional bodies of men and horses on his way. He knew that Agamemnon would be proud of the carnage. Ahead, as he neared the Mycenae camp, he saw Patroclus washing the shoulder of a wounded soldier. The soldier winced with pain, and Patroclus gave him a stick to bite on. When Patroclus backed away, Achilles saw that the man's arm was just barely attached at the shoulder. Patroclus took a knife and quickly severed the arm completely. The man spit out the stick as he passed out from the pain. Patroclus quickly cauterized the wound with fire before the man woke.

"Will he be all right?" Achilles asked as he approached.

"Yes," Patroclus replied. "More or less. It's difficult to live without an arm, but I think he'll live. Now, how did you fare?"

Achilles smiled and turned around so that Patroclus could inspect him.

"Come inside," said Patroclus. "We need to make sure that all that blood is someone else's and not yours. But your armor looks good and doesn't have any holes, so that's a relief."

Sometimes Achilles felt bad for putting Patroclus through the daily routine of worry. *But he knew what he was getting into when we lived together with Chiron for those years*, he told himself. *Chiron made sure that he knew, and Patroclus chose to stay with me.*

Achilles followed Patroclus into the tent. After placing his sword on a table, he unbuckled his armor and let it fall to the ground. Patroclus called for a servant to come and clean the armor. Then he grabbed a washbasin that was hanging over the fire. He dipped a rag into it and started scrubbing Achilles's back.

"That's hot," Achilles complained. "Too hot. It burns."

"You need hot water to bring anything that's festering to the surface," Patroclus replied. "I've kept you alive this long, haven't I?"

"I've kept me alive," Achilles said with a laugh. "You just make sure I don't die. There's a difference."

"Let's just each keep doing our part. The soldiers say that Locrist fell today. That's about half the time that it took to conquer Salamis. Agamemnon must be proud."

"Well, he shouldn't be too proud. He only wins because of the sheer number of the Mycenae soldiers. They're terribly trained and fight as bad. But, I suppose I have to give Agamemnon credit for his tactic. He leaves each kingdom intact—even lets the king keep his throne—so long as they swear to join him in war when he calls."

"From what I've heard," Patroclus said, "it's Queen Clytemnestra who came up with that idea. She calls the shots in Mycenae."

"She probably does take care of the bigger picture. Still, her strategy would mean nothing if Agamemnon wasn't able to win the individual battles. I don't always trust him, and I certainly don't always like him, but Chiron taught me to give credit where credit is due."

Patroclus continued to wash Achilles, his rag now pink with blood. After he finished with his body, Patroclus washed Achilles's hair with warm water. He inspected the scalp for any sign of a wound.

Oh, Patroclus, Achilles thought, *I like this part the best.*

When the cleaning was complete, Achilles put on a brown tunic and sat at the table. Patroclus poured him a goblet of wine and sat beside him.

"What's next, after Locrist?" Patroclus asked.

"Agamemnon is bringing his men back to Mycenae. He's right to give everyone a nice, long rest. I think he'll be satiated for at least a year. He doesn't have any formalized ties to Argos, Sparta, Ithaca, and Pylos. I know he'd like to have those kingdoms in his grasp, but I hope he's smart enough to realize that those four will stick together. He can't beat them combined."

"I don't think Clytemnestra would ever endorse an attack on any one of those," said Patroclus. "She's too smart. Besides, her parents are still the rulers of Sparta. They'll come to Agamemnon's aid if he ever needs it. Odysseus, king of Ithaca, will never stay away from a fight if both Mycenae and Sparta are together. And, of course, King Diomedes of Argos and Nestor of Pylos do whatever Odysseus does. You're right, the fighting probably is over."

"I want to take this time to form my own army," Achilles said. "I might not have this opportunity again."

"You'll be king of Phythia someday," Patroclus said. "You'll have your own army when you have the throne."

"No, that's not what I want. I hope to form a private army of mercenaries. Very well trained."

"You mean, an army for hire?"

"Yes. Fourteen thousand men for soldiers. One thousand for cooks, blacksmiths, and tailors."

"Fifteen thousand in a private army?" Patroclus asked. "How will you support all of them?"

"We'll support ourselves. I've thought it all out. I'll call them the Myrmidons."

"The ant men?"

"Yes. Like ants, each must carry more than his own weight. At the same time, each must also be dedicated to the group. That's why none of the men can be married—no families to distract them. We'll live together and train hard together. We'll be our own family. I'll command them, and you'll organize them. They'll be loyal to each other, to themselves, and to us."

"I don't think you'll have any trouble recruiting them. Your fame as the best warrior in all of Greece will do the recruiting for you. Many will want to learn the ways of Chiron. But you should include some more people trained in the art of wound healing. I can't take care of all fifteen thousand on my own."

"Of course. And you can teach them while I train the others."

"You'd better be careful how you talk about it," Patroclus said. "Agamemnon might feel threatened that a private army is out there. What's to stop your Myrmidons from conquering Mycenae itself?"

"I've already thought of that," Achilles answered. "This is the best part. The Myrmidons will be recruited from every kingdom in Greece. No Myrmidon will concede to attack his own people. This is how we show the kings that we'll work with them and not against them."

"We can start recruiting in Sparta when we go there next moon."

"Sparta?" Achilles said. "Why start there?"

"My father is sending me to Sparta," said Patroclus. "I'm representing the sons of the Argonauts at some sort of event. He told me to leave you back in Phythia, but you know I'd never agree to that. It's not that he doesn't like you, Achilles, but he seems to think that your presence will hinder whatever it is I'm supposed to be doing there."

"You don't know what's going on in Sparta?"

"Not exactly. I have a feeling it has something to do with the Princess Helen. She's about the age to marry. In any regards, I'm not going to compete for a hand I don't want. You can't leave my side—maybe that will give them all the idea to leave me alone."

"Sparta it is then," said Achilles. "No, you must never leave me behind. We Myrmidons will always stick together."

One moon later, in Sparta...

HELEN CHOOSES A HUSBAND

ELEN WAS QUITE accustomed to people staring at
her. In fact, she had taken to wearing a veil whenever she went out in public to disguise her beauty—she'd caused too many accidents by distracting horsemen. But as she sat on her throne in the great hall of
Sparta this day, she was in uncharted territory. She was
not accustomed to sitting in a room of staring men and
knowing that one of them would take her virginity later
that night.

King Tyndareus and Queen Leda stood by the door.
They welcomed all the suitors as they arrived, each in his
finest armor. Days earlier, it had been announced that this
would be Helen's choice: she would choose her husband
and the next king of Sparta. She felt a heavy weight and
thought, *What if I want an attractive man who would
make a terrible king? What if the best king is a brutish
bore whom I can't bear to have in my bed?*

Queen Clytemnestra entered through the door. After
her parents bowed to her, she embraced them. Becoming
queen of Mycenae, the most powerful kingdom in Greece,
had been good for Clytemnestra. She was much nicer. Helen realized that Clytemnestra was nice only because she

now had the upper political hand, but it did not bother her. She was glad to have a nice sister and cared little for politics. Clytemnestra visited Sparta often, and the two sisters had grown close, at least from Helen's perspective.

Clytemnestra sauntered down the middle of the great hall. She nodded to the suitors she recognized. Some of them bowed to her. She stepped onto the dais and sat right down on Tyndareus's golden throne, next to Helen.

"I'll borrow this chair for a while," Clytemnestra said. "Father is busy and we can talk."

"I need help," Helen replied. "Nobody has given me any direction, and I'm uncertain what I'm supposed to do. Am I to be first a wife or a queen?"

"That's what I'm here for. Now, let me look at you. I spent the entire ride from Mycenae praying to the Immortals that you'd wake up this morning with some kind of wart growing on your nose. But, alas, no. You're more ravishing than ever. You're the most beautiful woman in the world."

"It's a curse on a day like this," said Helen.

"It's a weapon that we'll use to get the best husband and the best king."

"Father is worried. He thinks that the losers will go to war with the winner over my hand."

"Agamemnon is also concerned," Clytemnestra replied. "We've worked hard to obtain peace within the states of Greece. But it's a tenuous peace at best. That's why your choice is so important. Now, let's consider the suitors."

By this time, a long line of men were waiting to be greeted by the king and queen. Their armor glistened in the light of the windows. All of them looked up at Helen on the dais. She could feel their desire. *But is it a desire to be married to the most beautiful woman in the world?* she wondered. *Or a desire to be king of Sparta? Probably both. Does anyone just want to be a husband?*

Clytemnestra began. "The man talking to the king is Elephenor, king of Abantes. He's a real bore. Absolutely no personality at all, a terrible prospect for both husband and king. After him is Menestheus, king of Athens. Menestheus is interesting, but the Athenians are not an agreeable group. Even if they were fine with him being king of both Athens and Sparta, they wouldn't accept you as their queen unless you renounce all ties to Sparta. So he's a risky choice."

"Who is that man behind Mother with the golden hair?" Helen asked. "It shimmers like the sun. He's very handsome. But he's dressed poorly in a tunic. Why isn't he wearing armor?"

"Oh, my dear, that's Achilles. Yes, the famous Achilles—the most fierce warrior in Greece. He's not wearing armor because he's not a suitor. His father, King Peleus of Phythia, has made it clear that he's to be the heir of Phythia with no ties to Sparta."

"Then why is he here?"

"Do you see the man standing next to him?"

"The handsome man with dark hair in the bronze armor? Yes."

"That's Patroclus. Achilles is here as his escort. Patroclus is son of Menoetius, the Argonaut. He's wealthy but of no royal lineage. He's known as a great healer. I've met him several times before, and he's extremely kind. I actually rather like him."

"He's handsome," Helen said. "And because he isn't royal already, perhaps he'd come without all the other entanglements. A healer would make a good king of Sparta."

"Unfortunately," Clytemnestra replied, "he's not a choice you can make. He and Achilles are men who choose to be with men—and these two have made it clear that they choose each other."

"Oh, my favorite male servant is like that," Helen said. "He chooses men."

"So does one of mine. I envy him. He just seems so happy all the time."

"Who is that enormous man in the back?" Helen asked.

"That's Ajax the Greater."

"Why is he called the Greater?"

"Because the man behind him, the one just as muscular but three heads shorter, is Ajax the Lesser. You don't want to marry anyone who's called the Lesser. And Ajax the Greater is sure to smother you if he rolls over in bed."

The men continued to enter the hall and sit. Clytemnestra told Helen about them all, including Protesilaus, Diomedes of Argos, Philoctetes, and Idomeneus of Crete.

"Who's the handsome one with the dignified way of walking?" Helen asked. "The one with silver armor and the well-trimmed beard?"

"That's Odysseus of Ithaca. He's very strong and extremely wise—too wise. He's clever and shrewd. I wouldn't trust him as far as I could throw him, which wouldn't be very far."

Helen's eye was caught by a man who had entered earlier and was now leaning against a wall not too far from the women. He was average by all accounts: looks, body, and stature. But he was well dressed, and Helen liked that he wasn't pretending to be impressive to the others.

"Who's that by the wall?"

"Helen, that's Agamemnon's brother Menelaus. He represents Mycenae. Since he's my husband's brother,

I know him well, of course. He's a good man. And, if I may be so bold, he's your best choice. He doesn't have his own kingdom and will work hard in Sparta. Plus, you need to think of the advantage that comes with two sisters marrying two brothers. This would bring peace between Mycenae and Sparta for generations. Our descendants will always be related."

"He looks ordinary."

"Ordinary is what you need. Father and I have talked at length about it. If you choose Menelaus, Father will abdicate the throne tonight—he likes the man that much. Mother and Father will move out of the palace and enjoy a retired life. You'll wake up the wife of Menelaus, the sister of Mycenae, and the queen of Sparta."

Well, that's something to think about, Helen mused. *Maybe it's better that my choice be made by Clytemnestra. It's nice to not have to feel the pressure.*

Now that all the suitors had arrived, Tyndareus and Leda took their places on their thrones. As Clytemnestra vacated the king's chair, Helen noticed that she winked at him knowingly. *There's more going on here,* she realized. *Perhaps the decision was already made weeks ago.*

"To all our friends," Tyndareus began, "welcome. It's no secret that Helen is the most beautiful woman in the world, and to marry her is to marry Sparta. She'll consider all of you. In the end, the choice will be hers. However, it's my sincerest hope that there be no sore losers here. Bloodshed is not beneficial in this situation."

Just then, Odysseus stood quickly, approached the dais, and said, "I have an idea, Great King of Sparta. An idea that will ensure peace whomever Helen may choose."

"What a shock," Tyndareus said sarcastically. "Odysseus has an idea."

The room erupted into laughter. Odysseus raised his hand and everyone fell quiet.

"All of us," Odysseus said, "all the suitors, that is, will take the Oath of the Quartered Horse—the most sacred and unbreakable oath we have. We'll all swear that we'll protect whomever wins the hand of Helen. If we all swear to protect that man, then none of us can fight against him."

"Wise, as always," said Tyndareus. "But, Odysseus, why would you suggest this? You yourself may not win her hand."

"With all respect to the beautiful Helen," Odysseus said, "I don't want to compete for her hand. Give me your niece Penelope, as we're already deeply in love. But I'll still take the oath as an act of solidarity."

Without another word, Tyndareus nodded and took some time to talk to his advisors. Then, everyone sat in silence as servants were sent to fetch a pure-white horse. The horse was still alive and it took great effort for several men to push her down to the floor. The horse bellowed in the pain of broken bones. Helen closed her eyes when Tyndareus drove a long knife into the middle of the animal. She opened her eyes to see Tyndareus nod at Ajax the Greater, who used a sword to hack the horse into four pieces.

The blood of the horse was collected in a washbasin. Each suitor now took his turn dipping his face into the basin. Upon raising out of the blood, each swore the oath before the Immortals and the others. Everyone, including Helen, knew of the Oath of the Quartered Horse. There was no way to break the oath without the Immortals killing all the people in whichever kingdom the traitor came from. *Nothing is really fair in this situation,* Helen thought. *Entire kingdoms are unknowingly pledged to possible doom because one man makes an oath. I don't want this weighing on my decision. I'll follow Clytemnestra's advice.*

The mess was then cleaned up, and a dinner began late in the night. Helen was exhausted when she finally announced that she would marry Menelaus of Mycenae. And, as Clytemnestra had told her, she woke that next morning as a wife and a queen.

Around the same time...

A TROJAN MARRIAGE

THE ENTIRE CITY of Troy was decked out in all its glory for the royal marriage of Prince Hector and Andromache of Thebe. Blue and silver flags flew from all the towers. The proud citizens dressed in their finest attire as they lined the streets, hoping to see the future king and queen of Troy.

Priam, the current king, and Queen Hecuba sat on their thrones. They watched as the huge wedding party in the great hall happened around them. King Priam looked with great satisfaction as he observed Hector and Andromache dancing together.

"She makes an excellent match for Hector," Priam said to his wife.

"Andromache is indeed lovely," Hecuba replied. "But she better also be fertile. Hector must continue your line."

"Hector is already the most revered soldier in all of Troy. There's no doubt he'll be the sire of many fine princes."

"Only if she's just as capable."

Priam looked past the newly married royals and noticed Prince Paris standing off to the side. As usual, he was surrounded by a flock of young girls. *He looks like he's enjoying himself*, King Priam thought.

"Now that he's been here over a year," Priam said, turning to Hecuba, "what do you think of our Paris?"

"I'm as elated as I was the day he first came back into our lives," said Hecuba. "Nobody alive wouldn't be happy to have a man as stunning as him for a son. Do you worry about him being back?"

"He's a fine young man and he's wasted no time fitting in with the family. But, is your question to ask me whether I'm scared of his birth prophesy?"

"It was."

"The prophesy said that the infant born to Hecuba that day would lead to the destruction of Troy. Well, he's no longer an infant and the danger has passed. The prophesy didn't say that a young man born on that day would be trouble for us. He's proven that he's loyal. I have no fear."

"The priest of Apollo doesn't agree with you," said Hecuba. "He thinks that you're putting too much faith in a technicality of words."

"The priest of Apollo won't even call him Paris even though we insist on it. He still calls him Prince Alexander."

"I worry about the priest. What if he should try to kill Paris? He certainly has a strong motive, and it wouldn't be too hard for him to find the opportunity."

"I agree with you," said Priam. "I've also worried some about the priest of Apollo taking matters into his own hands. That's why I've decided to send Paris away for a bit, at least until the priest calms down or disappears altogether."

"Perhaps it's time for the priest of Apollo to cross the river so that a new one may be anointed."

"Perhaps, my queen. Now, make yourself enjoy the feast while I speak to Paris."

Hecuba nodded and got up from her chair. Priam summoned a servant to fetch Paris. Priam watched as the servant attempted, with great difficulty, to get Paris away from the group of girls. Paris, dressed in blue, walked toward Priam's throne. *Hector is a great stallion*, Priam thought. *But Paris is a sleek racehorse. How different, yet how magnificent they both are.*

"Come, Paris," Priam said, "sit on your mother's throne and talk with me."

"How are you, Father?" Paris said as he sat comfortably.

"It's a good day for me. Hector is a man among men, and he has found the most fitting bride."

"Andromache is as beautiful as she is graceful," said Paris. "I hope to introduce a woman just like her to you someday as my own wife."

"I hope so, too. In the meantime, I have a quest for you, Paris. I want you to go to Greece with a small entourage."

"Greece? I've never been on the Aegean before, and I welcome the chance. What am I traveling there for?"

"A very long time ago, when I was just a boy, I had an older sister named Hesione. She was my favorite among all the members of my family."

"I've never heard anyone mention her," said Paris.

"That's because I forbid it—it's too painful for me. She practically raised me, you see. My own father was far too busy growing Troy into the great city it is today to show me much attention. I don't have any memories of my mother. Hesione was family to me."

"What does she have to do with Greece?"

"While I was still young, some Greeks came to Troy. They claimed they were here to offer assistance to my father, but he said the Greeks were just here to cause trouble. They believed that my father owed them some horses in exchange for their assistance, which, as I said, was never required. When my father refused to give them the horses, they left in the middle of the night. Heracles himself was with them."

"Heracles himself was in Troy? I never knew. That's amazing."

"Yes, except that he took Hesione as his prisoner in exchange for the horses that were never theirs to begin with. So is it with Greeks."

"What became of her?"

"She was given to Telamon, the king of Salamis. I want you to go to Greece and seek her out. It's been enough years without hearing of her. Find out if she's still a prisoner or if she has crossed the River Styx to the Underworld. I want to know what happened to her before I, too, make the journey across the river."

"I'll find out what I can, Father," said Paris. "Thank you for the opportunity."

"Paris," Priam continued, "be careful. The Greeks aren't like us. They're cunning and easily aggravated. Let your entourage protect you. And, always pray to Apollo. Apollo hates the Greeks."

"I'll leave as soon as I can," said Paris with much excitement in his voice.

A few moons after Prince Hector's wedding...

PARIS IN SPARTA

ARIS HAD BEEN seasick for most of the voyage across the Aegean. He was a bit disappointed and thought, *I'm definitely a shepherd and not a sailor.* However, being around a group of soldiers with lots of free time and no women gave him an opportunity to prove that he was as good with a bow as he always hoped. Growing up on Mount Ida, he'd become proficient shooting arrows at anything that threatened the sheep. Now he realized that he was as good as any of those who had been professionally trained by the army of Troy.

He'd been in Greece for one moon. They visited several kingdoms and heard the same story from every Greek they met: Hesione had fallen in love with Telamon, and they were living a happy life in Salamis surrounded by their children and grandchildren. According to the Greeks, there had never been a kidnapping by Heracles. And even if there had, Hesione was living a long and fulfilled life.

Paris and his entourage got close to Salamis, but they were never allowed to enter the city itself. At each attempt, they were intercepted by guards and told that there was a plague within the walls. King Telamon had ordered that nobody was to enter or leave. Consequently, Paris never saw Aunt Hesione in person. *Apollo controls all plagues, and he's on our side,* he thought. *I doubt anyone in Salamis even has the slightest cough, but what am I to do about it?*

Paris decided to visit Mycenae and speak with King Agamemnon himself about the situation. While on the way, they stopped at Sparta for food and a night of shelter. They arrived in the city and were escorted to the palace. That's where Paris noticed that the royal family must be in mourning. The statues were covered with black fabrics and there wasn't much activity.

Some sort of official approached the group as they entered the palace courtyard and said, "Greetings, travelers from the great City of Troy. Unfortunately, King Menelaus isn't here. His father died, and the king traveled to Crete with his brother, King Agamemnon, to attend the funeral rituals."

"I'm sorry to hear that," Paris said. "Perhaps we should just be on our way."

"No, stay," the official continued. "It's a long journey to Mycenae and, as I said, Agamemnon won't be there either. Stay and enjoy our Spartan hospitality. Eat and spend the night. Queen Helen didn't accompany her husband to Crete, and she's hosting a funerary dinner tonight. You would honor the king's father with your presence."

Paris thanked the official and was glad to be escorted into his own private guest quarters. Sparta was the first place in Greece that had offered him accommodations befitting a prince. He took a long nap on a most comfortable bed until he was summoned for dinner.

Paris washed quickly and put on his formal armor. Since the dinner was to be hosted by the queen herself, it was the correct protocol to follow.

When he entered the hall, he was surprised to see many people sitting at various tables. He was escorted to a table toward the side of the room by the same official who had met them earlier.

"Our apologies, Prince Paris," the official said. "It's customary during a time of mourning for the queen to show herself as generous and in complete control of the state. I'm sure you can understand that death tends to bring about the vultures, so to speak. The reason you're not being seated in a place of honor is so that she can placate others."

"I've been a prince for only a short while," Paris said. "But I can understand the concerns of the royal family at this time."

The official left, and Paris sat at a table filled with all sorts of foods. He saw his entourage of servants and soldiers seated at a table in the back of the hall. *I'd rather be with them*, he thought. Then his entire world changed when he saw the queen entering the banquet hall.

She's the most beautiful woman in the world, he realized. Helen wore a simple black tunic but was adorned with all manner of gold jewelry. Her several bracelets dangled and clanked together. *Her skin is perfection, and her hair is begging me to feel it.* He couldn't keep his eyes from exploring her body and the way she moved. She was beauty personified.

"It's true, is it not?" said a soft voice in his ear.

Paris turned to a servant woman who was filling his goblet with wine. However, when he looked closer, he recognized the woman and her flowing red hair from the cave.

"Aphrodite?" Paris said.

"Yes," she answered. "I've come to fill your wine and your soul. Didn't I tell you that I would bring you to the most beautiful woman in the world? There she is. You know, it's a great secret, but her true father is Zeus him-self. She's the only thing in this room more beautiful than you, Paris."

"What should I do?"

"That's up to you. I've brought you to this place, but what happens now will require a commitment from you. Will you make this commitment to beauty? We shall see. You'll eat and retire to your quarters, alone, when the dinner is complete. Then, when the moon rises, go out on your balcony. You will find a rope ladder. If you choose, climb the ladder. Helen of Sparta's quarters are directly above yours."

"She's not only married already but she's married to a king who's the brother of the most powerful monarch in Greece. None of this can happen."

"Yes," said Aphrodite, "she is married. And, surprisingly, she's rather happy about it. She finds Menelaus agreeable. But I know something that nobody else does—Helen isn't fulfilled at night. Menelaus isn't able to perform, and she longs for the passion that her beauty deserves. Go to her if you want. Or regret it."

Paris turned back to look at Helen. For the first time, their gazes locked. *I must look away or someone will notice the attraction.* He turned to look back at Aphrodite, but she was gone. He spent the rest of the dinner trying to look at Helen without seeming to look at Helen. He caught her doing the same thing to him. Each time their eyes met, his entire body felt alive in a way that it never had before.

After the eternity that was the dinner, Paris went back his balcony. He found that a rope ladder had already been attached to the balcony above. It was wound up in itself, concealing its existence. He couldn't wait for the moon. He unleashed the ladder, climbed up, and swung over the railing of the balcony above.

Helen was standing in the corner of her own balcony. She gasped when Paris swung over and his armor clanked against the stone side of the palace.

"How did you get up here?" she asked. "I saw you at dinner and knew that I should never be alone with you. I ordered both our rooms locked until the morning. You were to be escorted out of Sparta promptly at sunrise before my room was unlocked."

"There was a ladder," Paris said. *How odd,* he thought. *My first words to this glorious woman were about a ladder.*

"I instructed my servants to make sure there was no way for you to climb up here."

"Regardless, there was a ladder."

Paris could not tear his eyes from her. She had changed out of her regal mourning dress and wore only a flowing white gown. Her hair was down. She wore just a few pieces of gold jewelry. *Whatever she wears, she makes it look perfect.*

"Why did you want to avoid me?" Paris asked.

"You know why," Helen said, "just as much as I do. There's something extremely strong between us. But you also know, as well as I, that nothing can come of this. Menelaus—"

"Menelaus isn't here. And, according to you, your servants will think it impossible that we are together."

Paris took off his helmet and set it on the floor of the balcony.

"Put your helmet back on," Helen said. "You are a prince of Troy. Troy taxes the Hellespont, and my countrymen do not speak friendly toward yours. Two people from feuding cultures cannot fall in love."

"Who said anything about falling in love?" said Paris. "You're acting as if you'll leave your people and start a war between Greece and Troy. Nothing of the sort will happen. We're both people who can make our own decisions with the time we have."

"What are you proposing, then?"

"A love affair. Probably the greatest love affair each of us will ever have. How long will it take for Menelaus to return from Crete?"

"Two more moons. But you can't stay here that long— you can't even stay here longer than tomorrow. People will talk. Your own people of Troy will talk about your absence."

"That's why you'll come with me, in secret. You're supposed to be mourning, anyway. Just tell your servants that you need to go alone to see an oracle. Come with me on my ship. We'll have our time—the best time either of us will ever have. Then, when we land in Troy, I'll send you right back on a ship to Greece. You'll be back here before Menelaus even thinks of returning. It will be our great love affair and nobody need know."

But what if a love affair isn't enough? he wondered.

Days later…

HELEN AND PARIS ON
ANOTHER SHORE

ELEN STOOD ON the deck of the ship and saw her first glimpse of the towers of Troy as they rose beyond the beach. She'd been dreading this moment for days. Next to her, she overheard Paris arranging for the ship's captain to take her right back to Greece. Her stomach sank.

She thought about the night she met Paris. *That night in Sparta was the best of my life. Paris is as much a part of me as my arm or my leg.* She'd thought she'd have the entire voyage to have her fill of Paris. But his seasickness had other plans. *I need more than just that one night. I need more of his body.*

"Paris," she said to him as the captain walked away. "I still have time. As long as I leave before the next moon, I'll have time to return to Sparta before Menelaus. And, even if he gets back before me, it's not a stretch to believe that I was delayed on my journey to the oracle."

Paris grabbed her and kissed her passionately.

"We won't go to Troy, then," he said. "I'll take you to Mount Ida. There's plenty of time. You can see how I lived a simple life before I was a prince. You'll see why I honor my adoptive parents by insisting on being called by the name they gave me. You will learn who I am. We'll really come to know each other. Then I'll make sure you're on the fastest ship bound for Greece when the time comes."

I have to be careful. Helen told herself. *One more week easily becomes two more weeks. Then three. I must control my desire, not the other way around. I'm playing with fire, and I'm afraid that like it.*

Two moons later, in Greece…

MENELAUS VISITS MYCENAE

K ING AGAMEMNON LOVED few things more than conquering other kingdoms. One of those things he loved very much was his fourteen-year-old daughter, Iphigenia. He especially liked watching her skill on a horse. Clytemnestra didn't always approve of Iphigenia's love of riding, but Agamemnon encouraged it. He sat on a bench in the large courtyard of the Mycenae palace and watched Iphigenia jump over wine casks on her favorite mare.

Agamemnon's focus on Iphigenia was interrupted when a page entered the courtyard and ran over to him. "Your Highness," the page said. "King Menelaus of Sparta is here to see you."

"Send him out here," Agamemnon replied. "And find my guests Odysseus and Diomedes. They're somewhere in the palace. Tell them that Menelaus is here and I want to talk to all of them in the courtyard."

"Yes, Your Highness."

The page left. *Finally*, Agamemnon thought, *Menelaus has come. I've been waiting for this moment for weeks. Clytemnestra will be equally as happy. I knew it was wise to have Odysseus and Diomedes ready—well, it was Clytemnestra's idea to have them ready. But I had to make it happen.*

He continued to watch Iphigenia while Menelaus entered the courtyard alone. He walked over and sat next to Agamemnon on the bench.

"Welcome, brother," Agamemnon said. "It's a fine day in Mycenae. What draws you away from Sparta?"

"I need your help," Menelaus replied.

"Anything. You know that."

"Helen is missing. She went to seek comfort and advice from an oracle after our father died. She was absent from the palace when I returned from Crete. She should have been back weeks ago, and still she is nowhere to be seen. We've searched the mountains to no avail. Can you spare part of your army to help me search? I'm afraid for her. She may be dead somewhere."

She left him, Agamemnon thought. *She willingly left him. But that won't be good enough to energize Menelaus. I must remember what Clytemnestra told me about motivating him.*

"Menelaus, I thought you knew," Agamemnon said as he feigned surprise. "I would, of course, have told you as soon as I found out myself. However, I thought you knew. I didn't want to say anything to embarrass you. I felt it was best to just forget the whole thing. Clytemnestra wanted us to go to you, but I told her that—"

"Agamemnon," Menelaus interrupted. "What are you talking about? What should I have known?"

"Dear brother, it seems that Helen has been kidnapped."

"What! Kidnapped? How can this be? Who did this?"

"I heard about it myself from a Greek merchant. He saw her in the region of villages around Troy, in what they call the Troad. Now, she is across the Aegean, right outside the city of Troy. As you know, there's no mistaking Helen for anyone else alive. Many are talking about it."

"Troy?" Menelaus said. "What's she doing there?"

"She was seen with Prince Paris, Priam's son. There's a rumor that she left willingly and is in love with the man. But I know the truth. She was taken from your palace in Sparta while you were away mourning our father. What kind of foreigner enters a palace seeking hospitality and leaves with another man's wife? Shameful. Well, that's a Trojan for you."

"She's gone?" Menelaus said sadly. "For good?"

He doesn't understand it yet. He doesn't feel it yet.

"I'm afraid so," Agamemnon said. "The merchant told me that all of Troy is laughing at the impotent King Menelaus, who let the most beautiful woman in the world get away. Of course, I don't believe a word of that. Prince Paris either bewitched her or took her by force. Clytemnestra knows her sister well and said that Helen is too much in love with you to be bewitched. So she was surely kidnapped. Violently, most likely."

That should do it, Agamemnon thought.

After several long moments, Menelaus said, "Brother, I want her back."

"Of course you do. She's your wife. And she's in danger. You can't trust anyone from Troy."

"I don't care what it takes. I'll sail the Spartan army to Troy and rescue her from this enemy prince."

"The Spartan army will never be enough. Ah, how fortunate that my friends are here at this moment."

By this time, Odysseus and Diomedes were coming across the courtyard. Iphigenia, still riding, waved at them, and they waved back. Diomedes sat next to Menelaus on the bench, and Odysseus just sat right on the ground.

"My friends," Agamemnon began. "It seems that the situation with Helen is exactly as we feared. She has been kidnapped and is being held in Troy against her will. Menelaus has confirmed this. He wants her back."

"It's time that the Trojans pay for their boldness," said Diomedes. "Not just for Helen but for their control of the Hellespont. They're taxing our merchants into poverty."

"I agree, Diomedes," Odysseus said. "But the Greeks have always been reticent to go to war over Trojan taxes. The people fear that too many will die in the name of money. We must put focus entirely on Helen. The kidnapping of a beautiful young woman, who is a respected queen, is a serious offense. Every Greek will be outraged."

"Yes, Odysseus, as always you're correct," Agamemnon said. "I'll send word at once to all our allied kingdoms. Menelaus, you must return to Sparta and gather your treasury. We'll need money for ships. Clytemnestra will manage the logistics, she's good at that. After all, she'll want her sister returned."

"One more thing," Odysseus said. "We need Achilles and his Myrmidons."

"Absolutely not," Agamemnon said. "Yes, they've proven to be extremely well trained. But Achilles answers to no man. He can't be trusted. He already mistrusts me for some reason that I don't even know about. Clytemnestra's spies say that he mistrusts her, too."

"What if I told you that I have a way to gain his full support?" Odysseus said. "His Myrmidons will fight fiercely for us after I've had a chance to speak with him."

I don't like the idea of bringing Achilles with us to Troy, thought Agamemnon. *However, Odysseus is always right, and he must have a way to gain Achilles's support. The Myrmidons will make the war a quick affair.*

"You and Diomedes should leave for Phythia at once," Agamemnon said. "Get Achilles. Then go home and get your own armies. We'll rally at Aulis in six moons to board Clytemnestra's ships."

"I suppose this means that a life of peace is over," Menelaus said.

"Don't get cold feet, brother," said Agamemnon. "You alone can carry the flame of Helen and inspire the armies to fight for her."

He better play his part and not mess this up for the rest of us.

Shortly after...

THETIS SPEAKS WITH ACHILLES

T HE SEA WAS raging once again. Thetis walked calmly out of her cave and lifted her hand slightly, and the crashing waves retreated. She walked over sand and crushed seashells to the large flat rock she favored. Her long black hair flew in all directions as the wind billowed around her.

He's here, she thought without turning to look. *He's climbing over the shore. He's always dependable. A good soldier and an even better son.*

She turned and watched Achilles make his way over to her rock. He was dressed warmly, and she was briefly reminded that she sometimes made a terrible mother. She'd forgotten to consider how the weather might impact a mortal.

Achilles sat next to her. After he'd reached the rock mostly dry, she allowed the waves to resume crashing around them.

"I received your message," Achilles said. "I apologize for not coming sooner, but I had to make sure the Myrmidons were instructed on what to do during my absence."

"You've done well with them," Thetis answered. "I'm proud of your skill, not only with training them in battle but in managing the daily routines. Some of the other Immortals have commented to me on the efficiency of your camp."

"They're a dedicated group of individuals working together."

"Do you know why I've called for you?" Thetis asked.

"Not exactly. But I can feel that something is different in Greece. There's something unsteady in the air."

"Yes, we all feel it. The oceans are alive with news. Greece is preparing to attack Troy. Agamemnon and Menelaus are gathering all the kings and their armies. Clytemnestra is using her cunning and her considerable resources to build the largest fleet of warships ever constructed. The Immortals have begun to take sides. Apollo and Aphrodite are devoted to the Trojans with blind dedication. I'll never understand them. Athena and Hephaestus are backing the Greeks, as am I, of course."

"Athena is worth twice the force of Apollo and Aphrodite put together," Achilles said.

"Only you can get away with talk like that. Don't let Patroclus say such things. Apollo and Aphrodite will spite him and I need him to be alive to care for you."

"Patroclus is too smart to insult the Immortals."

"That's precisely why I need him to be with you."

Achilles laughed a little.

Yes, my son, she thought, *I know that Patroclus is the more sensible one.*

"They'll want my Myrmidons," Achilles said. "Agamemnon and the other kings will need us."

"Yes, and that's why I want to talk to you. Odysseus and Diomedes are on their way to Phythia as we speak. And now, after many years, the time as come for me to present you with your choice."

"Choice?"

"Yes, choice. You alone, among all the mortals, have the task of choosing between two fates. I give you this gift and this curse."

"But my fate should have been sealed when I was born, like all others."

"You aren't like others. You may choose between two fates. Your first choice is Greece. If you stay in Greece, you'll live a long life. You and Patroclus will grow old together and every day will be happy. I'll visit with you often, and one day you'll die an old man, sleeping in your bed. However, when you die, nobody will ever remember that you were here."

"And the second choice?"

"The second choice is Troy. If you go to Troy and join the war, you'll win many battles. You'll be hailed as the greatest hero Greece has ever seen. But know, you'll never see Greece again—you'll die in Troy before the war is over. However, when you die as such a young hero, your name will live for all eternity. Peoples from all parts of the world, peoples you can't even imagine, will know your name for all time."

"Would you be surprised to learn that growing old in Greece appeals to me?"

"I know you well, my son. I'm not surprised. All the Immortals expect that you'll seek glory for all time. But they don't know you like I do. I know that you cherish happiness and time with Patroclus."

Achilles sat in silence for many long minutes. They listened to the soothing sounds of waves crashing around them. Thetis realized that he was thinking deeply. She never understood why it always took so long for most mortals to make a decision. *The Immortals have all the time* in the world to ponder, but mortals need to make every moment count. Why waste so much time?

"What would you have me choose?" Achilles asked, eventually breaking the silence.

"I'm Immortal. The difference between you living to be thirty and you living to be ninety is a mere blink of an eye to me. However, I must admit that this particular blink of an eye means the world. I could not bear the reality that you won't come to visit me on this rock. Yes, I know that you must die, but if I could prolong that for a blink of an eye, then I would."

"It's settled, then. I will stay in Greece."

I'm glad, Thetis thought. *It's selfish of me to want him to live—I don't care what the others think of me. Everyone will be better off the more I prolong my grief over his eventual death.*

"But, Achilles," she said, "you must avoid Odysseus. He's too clever and will have the support of Athena. She knows that the Greeks would benefit from the Myrmidons. You must hide from him."

"The Myrmidons will expect me to lead them if they hear of war."

"They'll listen to you when you advise that this isn't their war. Instruct them to maintain their training schedules. I'll see that they're able to eat and live while you're in hiding."

"Where can I possibly go that Odysseus won't find me? He knows everyone. And those he doesn't know he drinks with until they tell him everything."

"Take Patroclus to the island of Skyros. My great friend, King Lycomedes, will devise a plan to hide you from Odysseus. I'll speak with him before you arrive. Lycomedes is almost as smart as Odysseus—almost. He's our best chance if you listen to his plan. However, if Odysseus does manage to discover you and speak with you, you must do your best to stick with your choice."

"I won't make any choice that undermines my dedication to you and to Patroclus."

Hopefully, Odysseus won't realize that and use it against you.

At the same time, on the other side of the Aegean...

PARIS AND HELEN
ARRIVE IN TROY

I N THE FEW moons since she'd left with Paris, Helen had
a recurring dream that they were on the back of a wild
chariot being pulled by four swift horses. The chariot
was racing toward a stone wall. She knew she could stop
the chariot if she would just jump from it, but her feet
were frozen next to Paris. When the chariot crashed into
the wall, she'd wake up.

On this morning, she woke to a day she had been dreading for over a week. They were still outside Troy, attempting to delay fate. However, Paris had decided that it was
time to give up on returning to Sparta and introduce her
to his family. Helen knew it was the right thing to do, but
she didn't know if she had the courage to go through with
it. She made sure to dress as simply as possible, and they
walked to Troy.

She'd seen the city from a distance, but never this close.
The walls were truly as massive as she'd heard. *That's good
for me*, Helen thought. *They're solid enough to hide behind for a long while*. And the city's enormous reinforced
gate was exactly as the merchants had described.

Helen and Paris had decided to walk, so as to appear humble, and they decided that Helen should not cover her face. Paris wanted the people to see that his risk was worth it since she really was the most beautiful woman in the world.

But as they walked through the gate and entered the city, Helen immediately noticed that, as usual, rumors had flooded Troy. People stopped doing their business and stared at the couple when they passed. Some of the children pointed at her. The loud streets grew suddenly quiet as the couple walked by.

Helen mustered as much dignity as she could. She held her head high. *After all,* she thought, *I'm a queen.* She nodded at the people, and some of them smiled back. As they walked, Helen took a chance to look at the fabled city. She was impressed with its obvious wealth and power. Nothing was in disrepair, and every person she saw was well dressed. She loved the design of the city—the buildings became taller as they walked higher and higher through the spiral streets.

At the top of the hill, they finally came to the palace of Priam and the royal family. Two long rows of Trojan guards with their giant blue plumes bowed as Paris and Helen walked through them. The great doors were open, and the pair entered the courtyard. Helen was shocked at how beautiful and perfect the courtyard seemed to be. Her Spartan courtyard was primitive and overgrown compared to this manicured space of green trees and stone walkways.

Eventually, they exited the courtyard and entered the great hall. Before them, four people sat on four giant chairs. Helen knew from their dress that she was surely looking at King Priam, Queen Hecuba, Prince Hector, and his wife, Andromache. Paris led her down the middle of the hall toward the four thrones. She made sure that she bowed lower than Paris when they arrived before the king.

"Father and Mother," Paris said, "I'd like to present the woman I intend to marry. This is—"

"This is Helen," Priam interrupted. "It could be nobody else but the queen of Sparta. You're truly as beautiful as they say."

"Thank you, Your Majesty," Helen said. "I'm grateful for your hospitality."

"Well now," Priam said, "that hasn't been decided yet. The question of whether we should be hospitable to you hasn't been answered. Tell me, Helen, are you here on your own account?"

"I wasn't, at first. I spent the first weeks in Troy undecided. But now, as I've seen your city and its people, I've decided to stay."

"You don't mention my son," said Queen Hecuba. "Isn't Paris the reason you should stay?"

"Of course, I love him as much as I've ever loved anyone. But I thought I would pay a compliment to your city and people—I apologize if it was a patronizing ploy for your affection."

"She's honest," said Priam. "At least there's that."

"Father," Hector said, "let's make this short. A ship leaves for Greece within the hour, and Helen should be on it. Send her back with an apology of gold coins and leave it at that."

Hector is as bold as his reputation, Helen thought. *Perhaps he really is the finest soldier in all of Troy.*

"Hector!" Paris said loudly. "I won't have you talk like that. Helen will be my wife, and I'll have no other. If she goes, I go."

"Would you sentence your city to destruction and death?" Hector said plainly.

"For the love of Helen," Paris replied, "yes."

"Come now, my boys," said Priam. "We don't know it will come to that. The Greeks stole Hesione from me, and now we've repaid the act. How will they dare to come and demand Helen's return?"

"When I was a boy," Hector said, "you told me to always think of Troy first and myself second. I'm compelled to state that you, my father, aren't thinking about Troy. The Greeks will attack."

"They can try," said Paris.

"They will attack," Hector repeated. "And they will win. They're more accustomed to war than we, as they've fought among themselves for far too long."

"But we have our walls," Priam said. "And we have their long journey across the sea to our advantage. Apollo will protect us as he always has."

"Apollo is also an Immortal to the Greeks," said Hector. "He could switch his loyalty without warning. Also, they'll surely have Athena on their side."

"Let me ask you, Helen," said Priam. "Will the Greeks attack us?"

How do I answer when I don't even know which side I'm on? she wondered. *Has the decision been irrevocably made that I should marry Paris and stay in Troy? Will people die over this? Can't I be content with Menelaus? I must go back to Sparta no matter how much I want to continue to share Paris's bed.*

"King Priam," Helen said, "I couldn't bear to watch people die over my happiness. As much as I would like more time with Paris, I'll be on the ship that Prince Hector has spoken of."

"No," said Paris, "you will absolutely not be on that ship. All of you, listen! Do any of you think that if the Greeks come, they come for Helen? Forgive me, my love, you truly are beautiful, but even you aren't worth a war that's sure to kill many Greeks. If the Greeks come, they come to end the taxes on the Hellespont and sack the city— taking all the wealth and distributing it among the kings of Greece. Whether Helen stays or not makes no difference to them at all. If Helen goes back to Sparta, they'll still claim that she was kidnapped. There will still be a war."

"Hector?" Priam said.

"Paris votes for her to stay, naturally. I still vote that she goes. Perhaps we can't avoid a war for eternity, but if Helen returns, we can avoid a war for as long as possible. We owe this to our people. If there be a reason for war, let it not be in any way our own fault."

"Hecuba?" Priam said.

"We hurt Paris enough when we sent him away to die as an infant. It is the will of the Immortals that he has returned, and it is the will of the Immortals that he be happy in love. My vote is for Helen to stay and become a Trojan princess."

"And Andromache?" Priam said.

"My heart stands with Paris, but my head stands with Hector. So, I'll take the side of my future children and vote that Helen should leave. You're lovely, Helen, and I'll miss the opportunity to be your sister. But I must give my unborn children the ability to grow up before they're forced to fight."

"It comes to me," said Priam. "A split family must be rejoined. I'll decide, and that decision will bind our family and all of Troy."

Priam sat in silence for several long moments. *Is he making the decision right now?* Helen wondered. *How odd. My father and Menelaus would excuse themselves and spend weeks considering the matter.*

Finally, King Priam clapped his hands and stood. A servant entered immediately.

Priam said loudly to the servant, "Go and exclaim to all of Troy that Prince Paris will marry Helen, a woman of royal birth from Greece. Also, all citizens are immediately directed to abandon their normal duties and take up the duties of the crown. The walls are to be inspected. The blacksmiths must produce weapons and armor. The granaries are to be filled to the top. All stores must be secured, especially those for wine and clothing. Inspect the wells inside the city and secure the water supply. Tell the city that we prepare for war."

Three moons later, back in Greece...

ON SKYROS

ODYSSEUS AND DIOMEDES had been in Phythia for less than a day when they learned, from King Peleus himself, that Achilles wasn't in the city. They found the Myrmidon camp and discovered that Achilles wasn't there either. However, they learned in a camp tavern that Achilles had been put into hiding by his mother.

I'd hoped to get to him before his mother could, Odysseus thought. *This might be a bit tricky.* "She's an Immortal," he said. "In order to find him, we must think like an Immortal."

"Impossible," Diomedes said. "She'll have him hidden somewhere that she knows about. And since she's Immortal, she knows about a lot of places."

"That's it!" Odysseus exclaimed as they rode out of the Myrmidon camp on horseback. "She can only have him in a place that she knows about. Thetis is a relative of Poseidon. She must always stay close to the seashore. She won't have him anywhere on land. An island—that's where he is. It makes the most sense that she has him in a place where she can see from all sides."

"There are hundreds of islands with thousands of caves," Diomedes said.

"Skyros—he's on Skyros."

"Why Skyros?"

"A few years ago, King Lycomedes came to Ithaca. We got drunk together. He bragged that his island was protected by an Immortal woman. He's clever, and she'll know that. I'll bet my favorite dog, Argos, that he's on Skyros."

"How will we get there? Surely she'll see us coming and destroy whatever vessel carries us. I'm telling you, Odysseus, even you can't outsmart an Immortal."

"We'll see about that," Odysseus replied. "We'll disguise ourselves as beggars."

"Why would any beggar take a hard journey to an island when he could do just as well begging on the mainland?"

Diomedes found a hole in my plot, Odysseus thought. *Good for him! I guess even I can make the rare mistake.* "Good point," he said. "We'll be shipwrecked fishermen. Come, we must buy the oldest and junkiest boat we can find."

Later that night, a small fishing vessel that was barely held together washed up on the shore of Skyros. The two fishermen inside the boat cursed loudly as they attempted to bail water and continued to sink into the sea. They looked rough and were drunk. They continued cursing at each other while a few Skyrosian men rescued them and brought them to the island's city. To the sounds of laughing guards, they were escorted inside the palace to receive hospitality from the king for the night.

Odysseus maintained the charade of drunkenness as he held on to Diomedes and entered a hall full of people who were long into their dinner. The two were shown to a place of least honor at the back of the room. Odysseus looked around at the wide tables of feasting townspeople. In the front of the room he saw King Lycomedes sitting and holding court while he ate and drank from more than one goblet of wine. Behind him, elevated on a stage, his daughters performed a dance in flowing skirts. Several musicians played off to the side of the room.

Oh! The famous dancing daughters of Lycomedes! Odysseus thought. *They're lovely. But get back to the task. Where is he?* "I don't see him anywhere," Odysseus said quietly.

"I don't see Achilles, either." Diomedes replied.

I'm not looking for Achilles, fool, Odysseus scoffed in his head. *You can't find Achilles by looking for Achilles.*

Odysseus carefully studied each townsman, guard, and male server in the room. He paid special attention to anyone who wore any sort of head or face covering. *I don't see him, but he has to be here.*

Then Odysseus saw the clue he was looking for. Directly across from them, a stray dog had snuck into the room. *Cook something that smells good, and the smartest dog will always gain access,* he thought with a laugh. He watched as several servants kicked at the dog to keep it away from the tables. The dog whined and didn't give up trying until another servant, a young man from the front, walked all the way back and bent down. He picked up the dog and brought it to the corner of the room. He proceeded to fill a plate with food and set it down in front of the dog.

There he is, Odysseus realized. *Patroclus. And, of course, his heart has betrayed them.*

Without any warning, Odysseus turned and grabbed a sword off the guard standing behind him. He jumped onto the table and ran, through the dishes, toward the servant who was feeding the dog. The entire room stopped, quieted, and stared.

"This servant stole from me!" Odysseus yelled in disguise. "He must pay! He has taken my money!"

Odysseus jumped from the table and was within striking distance. Patroclus, disguised as the servant, looked at him with horror. Then screams erupted from the front of the room. One of the dancing daughters, still in a flowing skirt, had also jumped onto the table. Running as fast as a deer, she retrieved a large knife from a cut of meat. All at once, the flowing skirt flew away and the knife went spiraling through the air toward Odysseus. With perfect aim, the knife knocked the sword out of his hand. Now the room erupted into gasps as people began to realize that the dancing daughter was a man—and not just any man. The gasps turned to exclamations as Achilles revealed himself.

I was right to look for Patroclus! Odysseus said to himself. *Achilles made such a beautiful woman that I might never have known unless I'd had the idea to seduce the daughters!*

Achilles stood in the middle of the table, half-dressed as a woman with bright paint on his face. He reached up and pulled a large pin from his head, allowing his brilliant gold hair to be freed from its braid. His eyes were fierce, daring Odysseus to make another move. But Odysseus, instead of reaching for another sword, started laughing.

By this time, Diomedes had grasped the situation and jumped onto the table as well. He approached Achilles and whispered into his ear. The stunned audience watched as Achilles jumped off the table, grabbed the accused servant, and walked out of the room with him and the two ragged fishermen.

"Clever Odysseus," Achilles said. "My mother will be furious that you outsmarted her. So will King Lycomedes. He thought this disguise was impossible to penetrate."

"It turns out," Odysseus said, "it's easy to hide a mighty warrior's strength. But most difficult to hide true humanity. I apologize, Patroclus, for attempting to kill you."

Patroclus didn't respond. He stood with them until he noticed that the dog had followed them out. Patroclus bent down to soothe him.

"I know why you're here," said Achilles. "Tell Agamemnon that this is one war the Myrmidons will miss. There's nothing you can say to persuade me. The Myrmidons and I will not fight in the war for Helen."

"It's not all about Helen," Odysseus said. "You must know that."

"Of course I do. But fighting over tariffs that a foreign land has enacted over its own domain isn't a noble fight. Nor is going to war in order to rob a city of its wealth. We will not fight."

Now, it's time to release the snare, Odysseus thought. "I understand," he said slyly. "Actually, I completely understand. So we'll just be on our way. Patroclus, are you ready to sail?"

"What are you talking about?" Achilles said loudly with a mighty laugh. "How could you presume that Patroclus, of all people, would go with you when I would not?"

"Patroclus has no choice," said Odysseus. "He made the Oath of the Quartered Horse. He must go, or die right here, right now."

Odysseus watched as Achilles's face went from laughter to sheer hate. He kept an eye on Achilles's hands. They curled into fists. Patroclus now stood, leaving the dog, and confronted Odysseus with an equally hateful stare.

"That oath," said Achilles, "was to protect the husband of Helen from the other suitors."

"Incorrect," Odysseus replied. "The oath, if you recall, was to protect the husband of Helen from all threats, no matter whom that threat may come from. Menelaus is the husband of Helen. Going to war is a threat to his survival. Patroclus has no choice but to join Diomedes and me. What you and the Myrmidons do is your own business, but Patroclus is now Agamemnon's business."

I'm surprised by my own intelligence for the first time, Odysseus thought. *Is there nothing sacred to me? I'm exploiting these men. But the greater good must always be the greater motive. Without the Myrmidons, thousands will die. Patroclus is one man.*

"All right, Odysseus," Achilles said sadly. "I can't fight your wit. You knew that you'd have me before you even left Mycenae to look for me. The Myrmidons, Patroclus, and I will join your fight against Troy. However, clever Odysseus, you'll need the aid of all the Immortals if something should happen to Patroclus."

"Fair enough," Odysseus said. "Now, Diomedes, accompany these fine men back to their Myrmidon camp. I'll stay here a bit longer. There might be more to learn about King Lycomedes and the Skyrosian soldiers he may be hiding from us. Some drunken servants are sure to tell all. I'll meet you in the camp tomorrow."

Later that night...

ACHILLES CONTEMPLATES

*I*s *this fair? Mother, I didn't get a chance to make my own choice. Odysseus and Agamemnon made it for me. I'm forced to sail to Troy, where you said I'll die. Yes, my name will now live forever in all countries, but I'll still die. Patroclus may probably die—he is too human to survive a war of this magnitude.*

Is this fair, Mother? The choice was supposed to have been mine. I suppose that some will say I still have a choice. Is my choice now to abandon Patroclus—to send him to Troy and his death alone? Why should I live a long life in Greece without him?

My choice has been hijacked, and I'll never forget that.

Three moons later…

THE GREEK FORCES GATHER

GAMEMNON HAD BEEN living in a tent at the harbor of Aulis for more than two moons. Daily, he climbed a tall hill next to the port to survey the Greek war machine. Below him, on the flat plain and the beach, thousands of tents composed a movable city of men. Smoke rose from cooking fires, and the sound of life was everywhere. *I love all this*, Agamemnon thought.

The tents of Mycenae and Sparta were in the middle. Odysseus's Ithacans and the tents of Argos, under Diomedes, were close to the center. Nestor's tents from Pylos sat next to the enormous collection of portable dwellings under the control of Idomeneus, king of Crete. The tents of Lokris, under Ajax the Lesser, and Salamis, under Ajax the Greater, stood on the perimeter, surrounding the tents of Athens and the many other city-states of Greece.

However, the greater sight was the spectacle of ships anchored in the water. One thousand ships had been built with Spartan wealth and Clytemnestra's extraordinary ability to organize. Their painted masts sparkled in the sunshine. Small boats carrying supplies were being rowed between the shore and the ships. The plain and the beach— even the Aegean itself—were vibrating with the energy of human activity. *Excellent. Just excellent*, Agamemnon thought. *It's now time to call the war council.*

He was about to descend the mountain when he noticed something strange. The black tents of the Myrmidons, which had usually occupied the ground behind the Ithacans, had been moved a long way back inland. A large vacant space occupied the area between the Myrmidons and their nearest camp neighbors.

Achilles is at it already, Agamemnon mused. *He's not content being part of us and just has to conduct his own affairs apart from his countrymen. How will we endure him? How will he endure us?*

He huffed down the hill and was heading toward his own camp when he ran into Diomedes. "When did Achilles decide to part from the group?" Agamemnon asked. "I suppose he's too special to sleep next to us."

"Yesterday, Agamemnon," Diomedes replied. "But he didn't want to go—we made him. He's constantly drilling and training those men. Night drills, morning drills, midafternoon drills, between-bites-of-breakfast drills. It was driving us crazy. Odysseus finally talked to him, and he agreed to move away a bit. How much training can one soldier take? I fear that the Myrmidons will soon get fed up and cause a mutiny."

"I doubt it," Agamemnon said. "He picked a certain type of man who's devoted to this rigor. It's practically their religion."

"And Patroclus is just as bad," Diomedes continued. "He has started some sort of school to train wound healers. He recruited from all of us. I lost ten of my best soldiers to his school."

"Wound healers? But the only people who need wounds healed are the kings. Why waste resources on wounded soldiers? Put them out of their misery as has been done since the beginning of time."

"That's exactly what I told him. But Patroclus called me a barbarian and took the men anyway. But what can I expect from a man who feeds stray dogs at a banquet?"

"All this will be behind us soon enough," said Agamemnon. "Go and find Odysseus. Raise the call for a war council."

Diomedes showed an excited face and ran off toward the tents of Ithaca. As Agamemnon entered his own tent, he heard the bells summoning the kings to him. He instructed that the council flag be flown in front of his tent.

The kings arrived, one by one, and took a seat at the war council table. Agamemnon could not decide if he wanted Achilles to be near him, where he could keep an eye on him, or far from him, where Agamemnon felt safer. But he didn't have to worry about that for long, as Achilles entered and refused a chair at the table. He sat in a chair near the doorway.

As upsetting as he is, he certainly does look the part, Agamemnon thought. *He's magnificent.*

"My friends," Agamemnon addressed the group, "let us begin this first war council. We have wine from Salamis and women from Aulis waiting for us when we're through. So I'll be brief. We'll sail for Troy tomorrow."

Several of the men clapped, and others laughed out loud with pleasure. Agamemnon calmed them by raising his hand.

He continued. "We'll council on my ship as we get near the city. Our plan, basically, is to land on the beach, all one hundred thousand of us, and storm the city. We want the heads of Priam, Hector, and Paris. Helen is to be taken alive. Everyone else should be killed. Then we'll enjoy Trojan wine and women."

"I have a concern," said the deep voice of Achilles as he remained seated. "Is it true that your own priest, Calchas, went to the Oracle of Delphi and discovered that the war will last ten full years?"

The tent grew silent, and all eyes darted toward Agamemnon. *That damn priest. Why can't he keep his mouth closed?* Agamemnon said to himself. *I thought I was the only one he told about this. Now, they'll all get spooked.* He smiled and cleared his throat.

"I've heard that rumor as well," he said. "I suspect that Calchas himself started it. He's a gifted priest but likes fame. He revels in the news and panic he can spread. Pay no attention to him. Is there anything else?"

"Yes," Achilles continued. "It doesn't really matter if Calchas is right or if it's conjured gossip. What matters is that the walls of Troy have never, ever been breached. They're tall, wide, and strong. What happens if the war isn't over in a day? I've noticed that none of you have prepared for a long affair. There are very few blacksmiths and tailors in your camps. I haven't noticed any stores of grain going onto the ships. You don't even have breeding pairs of horses and cattle to replenish the animals that grow old. None of you have stores of wine."

"It takes years for a horse to grow old, Achilles," Agamemnon argued. We'll be back in Greece before a mare can complete her time. And there's plenty of wine in Troy. Achilles, relax and enjoy the journey. My friends, don't listen to this alarmist talk."

"I don't care if you're my friend or not," Achilles said. "Friends can run out of food and weapons just as enemies can. I've planned, and the Myrmidon ships will be well supplied. I don't know what the rest of you good kings can accomplish in one night, but I encourage you to try—for your soldiers' sakes."

Achilles stood and straightened his tunic. He ran his fingers through his hair and nodded at the kings. He started to leave the tent.

There's no doubt he's much better at this than anyone else here, Agamemnon thought. *Why didn't Clytemnestra insist on more supplies? Curious.* "Achilles, wait," he said. "Please, stay and enjoy the wine. We've had a disagreement, that's all. I pray to the Immortals that we'll never disagree again."

"I pray the same," said Achilles in the doorway. "Thank you for the invitation, but my men have organized an evening of battle games, and I wish to partake. Good night."

That same night, in Troy…

PRIAM'S PRIEST HAS A VISION

THE PRIEST OF Apollo left his temple and walked up the stone path toward Priam's palace. His appearance betrayed the fact that he hadn't slept in three nights. He'd been plagued with terrible dreams. The priest had spent all day praying to Apollo and had finally received some information in the form of a vision.

He had full access to the palace, and it wasn't difficult to walk past the guards and enter the courtyard. *Dinner must be over*, the priest thought. *I see Hecuba and Andromache on a walk with Helen. It's good that they've befriended her. The poor girl—an unknowing pawn to bring about the prophesy of Alexander's birth. Hopefully my news can change all of that. She has so much beauty, but she may incur the wrath of an entire country. Which country remains to be seen.*

The priest entered the great hall and, seeing it empty, walked up a winding stone staircase. He knew that Priam would be on his parapet, overlooking everything he protected. The customary breeze of the Troad gave the night a perfect temperature. The priest made his presence known and bowed to Priam.

"Yes, priest," Priam said. "What do you have for me tonight?"

"Are we alone?" the priest replied. "It's important that we be most alone. I have news of great importance that will cause enormous harm to Troy if it's known."

The priest watched as Priam looked around the parapet. Both of them also peered over the edge of the stone rail to make sure nobody had their head out an open window.

"Yes, what is it?" Priam said.

"I have a message from Apollo himself. It has been made known to the Immortals that the great city of Troy will never fall unless two conditions are met. These conditions are more powerful than the prophesy that Alexander, I mean Paris, will cause the destruction of Troy. All we need to do is make sure that these two conditions are never accomplished."

"Did he tell you of the conditions? If not, then you won't sleep until he does."

"Yes, of course, I'm his faithful servant. First, the arrows of Heracles must be brought to Troy and used to kill the heir to the throne."

"The poisoned arrows of Heracles?"

"Yes, the very ones.

"Where are they?" Priam asked.

"It's good news, Your Highness. The arrows are considered lost."

"Still, they might be somewhere. And if they are somewhere, Odysseus is sure to find them."

"But he won't know to find them because we're the only ones to know the message of Apollo. I believe the arrows of Heracles are not a high concern. Plus, even if the Greeks obtain them, they'll have to meet the second condition, and that will be impossible."

"What's the second condition?"

"Have you heard the name of Achilles?" the priest of Apollo asked.

"He's the warrior—yes? The great soldier of Greece."

"The second condition is that Troy won't fall unless the son of Achilles sets foot inside Troy and kills the king."

"And, why is this impossible? Surely this Achilles is virile and, no doubt, well built. If the prophesy is true, then we must fear even an illegitimate son. Isn't it possible that some woman has had a son by him?"

"I've made it my business to know everything about the Greeks, and especially their leaders. No, it's not possible. Achilles is a man who has chosen a man."

"Really?" Priam said. "Interesting. I've known a few of these men in my time. They make dedicated soldiers because they're so fierce to protect their own."

"Still," continued the priest, "even a man such as this could be made to lie with a woman if a victory depended on it. We must keep the two conditions secret so as not to give the Greeks any idea of how to win."

"Of course. The secret of the conditions will die with both of us in our beds, in a secure Troy."

The two men stood in silence and looked out over the city. The priest noticed the torches of the winding streets as they flickered in the wind.

How strange, he thought. *The wind seems to have shifted. This is the wrong time of the year for that. Perhaps I'll dream about that tonight, but hopefully I'll enjoy a night of much-needed rest.*

Two weeks later, at Aulis on the Greek shore...

THE WRONG WIND

ODYSSEUS WALKED WITH determination through the wind and toward Agamemnon's tent. The fleet had still not yet left the port of Aulis. Two weeks earlier, on the day they were supposed to leave, the Greeks woke to gale-force winds pushing giant waves toward the harbor. No ship, even one with rowers, was able to overcome the waves and get to open water. The entire Greek fleet had, essentially, been grounded. The winds persisted day after day.

The men in the camp were growing restless as supplies dwindled and spirits dropped. *Finally, maybe something is going to be done about this,* Odysseus thought. He walked into Agamemnon's tent and sat at the table. There were four others present: Agamemnon, Menelaus, Diomedes, and the old priest Calchas. *I'm uneasy around that priest. Athena favors him, and I know that I could never persuade him if I needed to.*

"Good," Agamemnon said, "everyone is here."

"What's this about?" Diomedes said. "Why all the secrecy?"

"I have a message to deliver," Calchas began. "The message is for Agamemnon, but had I delivered it to him alone, I would have surely been killed."

"I'll kill you now," Agamemnon said, "if you don't get on with it. Do you know something about the wind?"

"Yes," Calchas continued. "I've spent days communing with the Immortals. However, Agamemnon, I'm warning you that you won't like the message."

"Get on with it," Agamemnon said.

"You're a warrior king. What's more, the Immortals know that deep in your heart you desire to be the greatest of all warrior kings. Because of that fate, you were expected to dedicate your firstborn son to Ares and your firstborn daughter to Artemis. When your son Orestes was born, you did your diligence and brought him to the temple of Ares for dedication. However, when Iphigenia was born, you didn't dedicate her to Artemis. Is what I say true?"

All eyes went to Agamemnon. He was growing visibly uncomfortable in his chair. "It was Clytemnestra," Agamemnon said. "She insisted that Iphigenia be dedicated to Aphrodite so that she may grow in beauty as Clytemnestra herself had not."

"Whatever the reason," Calchas said, "this was a grave oversight. Artemis is furious with you and waited for the most opportune time to demand retribution. Unfortunately, her perfect time is our worst time. Zeus's mortal son, Sarpedon of Lycia, has joined the Trojans. Artemis has easily persuaded Zeus to keep the strong winds blowing toward Aulis."

"There must be something we can do," Diomedes said. "Should we build a temple to Artemis on the shore of Aulis? Perhaps we dedicate our fleet to her?"

"No," said Calchas. "Artemis is quite clear. She was slighted and will accept only one act—an act of true repentance. You must bring Iphigenia here and sacrifice her to Artemis."

Odysseus looked at Agamemnon and saw that his eyes were filled with rage. His body was stiffening as he struggled to stand. *This isn't good. Agamemnon loves that girl. She might be the only thing he truly loves.*

Menelaus put his hands on his brother's arms in order to calm him. But Agamemnon shouted with rage. "This discussion is over! Over!" He stormed out of the tent.

"Is there no other way?" Odysseus asked Calchas.

"No," Calchas said.

"Agamemnon loves Iphigenia," Menelaus said. "And he fears Clytemnestra. Do not, any of you, ever repeat that!"

They left the tent frustrated and confused. Agamemnon wouldn't talk to any of them for the next two moons as the wind continued to blow fiercely against them. The situation in the Greek camp was dire with impatience, and Odysseus began to contemplate how to obtain Iphigenia and kill her himself. Then, when restlessness caused the soldiers of Mycenae to stage an open revolt, Agamemnon called for the four others. *Finally*, Odysseus thought. *I've had a solution ready for days.*

"How will this be done?" Agamemnon asked in his saddest and most dejected voice. "Clytemnestra will never agree to this."

"I have it figured out," Odysseus said. "We'll send a message to Mycenae proclaiming that Achilles wants to marry Iphigenia before he leaves for war. I know Clytemnestra. She craves for her daughter to have beauty and marry the most handsome man in Greece. She'll send Iphigenia to us immediately."

"Clytemnestra will never fall for it," said Agamemnon. "She knows of Patroclus."

"Many men who choose men also take a wife," Odysseus said. "It will make sense that Achilles, future king of Phythia, will need a wife to continue the line. Patroclus already understands this, as will Clytemnestra. It's the only way I can think of to get Iphigenia here. She would have no other legitimate reason to visit our encampment without a chaperone. Only a journey to her husband's bed is a reason for her to travel alone."

"What if Clytemnestra demands to attend the wedding?" Diomedes asked. "Surely, she will."

"No, she won't," Odysseus said. "Agamemnon, you know as well as I that she must stay in Mycenae to keep a steady hand on your throne. If both of you were gone during this time, the throne would be taken by force. I speak the truth, yes?"

Agamemnon didn't say anything. He just nodded. *He looks so sad*, Odysseus reflected.

"I'll arrange the messenger," Odysseus said. "But we must make sure that Achilles doesn't hear of this. He won't like that we're using his name in this manner."

The messenger was sent. Then, hours later, Agamemnon got cold feet and sent a second messenger to tell Clytemnestra to ignore the first messenger. However, Odysseus anticipated Agamemnon's regret. He sent a third messenger to intercept and kill the second messenger. Finally, the only message that Clytemnestra received was the original statement of marriage between her beloved daughter and the most eligible man in the entire country.

Iphigenia arrived the next day. Odysseus was heartbroken that she arrived already wearing an elaborate wedding dress. *There's nothing I can do about that*, he thought. *The greater good of appeasing Artemis is more important than the life of a young girl. My solutions are never easy, and often an innocent person dies. However, I'm saving thousands.*

The four kings and Calchas arranged for Iphigenia to meet them on Agamemnon's favorite hill. Odysseus noticed that Agamemnon wouldn't look at his daughter, even though she attempted several times to get his attention. *She's upset that he's not happy on her wedding day. They're close, this father and daughter.*

Calchas gave Agamemnon a large knife. He grabbed his daughter, slit her throat, and softly laid the gurgling girl on the ground. *I'm surprised he didn't cry out,* Odysseus thought.

But within the moment, there was a tremendous cry.

"Stop!"

All of them turned to see Achilles bounding up the hill. He was followed by Patroclus. Achilles ran to Iphigenia. There was an unbelievable amount of blood pouring from the girl, her wedding dress instantly showed stains. Odysseus watched the life drain out of her eyes, as her panicked expression turned into nothingness.

"I'm too late," Achilles said. "How dare you use my name? Agamemnon, you're lower than the insects."

"How did you know?" Odysseus asked. *I have to know.*

Patroclus said, "I discovered from my healers that the four kings were meeting without the others. I finally got to the truth, but I'm also too late."

He's using his healers as a spy network, Odysseus realized. *I give you great credit, Patroclus, but it won't happen to me again.*

"I'll send word to Clytemnestra," Achilles said. "Mark my words, Agamemnon, you'll pay for what you have done to your daughter in my name. And from now on, I'll do what I want with the Myrmidons. We'll fight when I say to fight. There's no need to brief me on any of your plans. If it were just you, Agamemnon, and your men, I would leave now. But as it is, the Myrmidons will stay in this fight only to make it shorter and save Greek lives. Do not talk to me again, Agamemnon."

Odysseus saw a stream of Iphigenia's blood reach toward Agamemnon's sandaled feet. Then, at the instant that the blood rose above his sandals and touched his bare flesh, the wind swirled around. Odysseus and the others were practically blown off the hill as the gale blew across the Aegean and toward Troy.

One week later, in Troy…

HELEN MAKES A CHOICE

SPARTA WAS OFTEN foggy, with hot summers and cold winters. The climate of Troy was much more agreeable. Helen started leaving her quarters often to enjoy the sun and cool breezes of the palace courtyard. She sat, alone, on a bench and watched the other members of the royal family congregate.

There is where Paris and I were married, she thought. *Right under that tree. The family seemed happy then, but who knows what happiness is anymore.*

Hecuba came out of the palace and nodded toward Helen. Helen returned the nod, and Hecuba crossed the courtyard to inspect a garden of flowers that her daughter Cassandra was studying. With his minor wives, Priam had many children. But only those he had with Hecuba really mattered.

How do some of Priam's other sons feel about Paris arriving out of nowhere and outranking them? Helen wondered. *Still, they have all been mostly cordial toward me, probably at Priam's insistence. He seems to like me and shows me proper respect. After all, no matter what has happened, I'm still a queen of a long royal lineage.*

But their wives, and the other women of Troy, all hate me. I can sense it.

Paris and Hector had been away from Troy for just over two moons. They were on a mission to recruit support from other cities around the Troad. Paris's absence made for long, lonely days and even longer, lonelier nights for Helen. She missed his daytime smile that melted her heart and his nighttime body that melted the rest of her. *No matter what people say about Paris, he's a devoted husband.*

The sound of hooves on stone echoed through the courtyard as Andromache entered on her white horse. *She looks as magnificent on that animal as her husband does,* Helen thought. *Was there ever a more perfect pair?*

Andromache jumped off her horse without assistance from the nearby wranglers. She walked deliberately toward Helen and sat down next to her on the bench. Helen was always uneasy when she was alone with Andromache. She respected the Trojan princess so much that she desperately wanted to avoid disappointing her.

"Good afternoon, Helen," Andromache said.

"Good afternoon," Helen replied. "How was your ride?"

"Productive. I'd received word that Hector and Paris are returning today. I rode out to meet them as they approached the city. They've gone to brief the army and will meet us for dinner."

I'm so glad, Helen thought. *I'm so tired of being alone here. I miss our private time together.*

"Did they say if their journey provided allies for Troy?" Helen asked.

"Yes. They've been able to make alliances with many cities in return for free access to the Hellespont. They were especially glad that Sarpedon of Lycia will lead the Trojan army directly under Hector. We need leadership of this caliber if we're to beat the Greeks. They have so many famous commanders, and we have just Hector."

Helen had wanted to ask Andromache a question since the night that Paris and Hector left. But she always avoided it. Now, Helen realized it was this time, or never.

"Andromache," Helen said, "I need to ask you a question. This question will set me on a course. I need you to be honest with me."

"I know," Andromache said. "I could see it on your face since the men left. You want to know if I think you should run away and return to Menelaus."

"Yes, that's my question. Please, you must answer. Tell me, what do you feel in your heart. If you say it, I'll leave the palace within the hour and hide by the shore. When the Greeks arrive, I'll run to Menelaus."

"Helen," Andromache said, "I believe that you would. And I respect you for your willingness to do whatever you can to spare Trojan lives. But we both know that your actions will have no impact on whether or not there's a war. This war is about so much more than both of us even comprehend."

"I know!" Helen said, raising her voice a bit. "Then why, if it's not my fault, do the other women avoid me? I feel hated in the city."

"I'll tell you why. The problem is that you're so ambiguous about your life, and it drives us quite mad."

"What do you mean?" Helen asked.

"I mean," Andromache said, "that we can't decide if you wanted to run away with Paris or if you were, indeed, kidnapped. I don't think that even you know the answer. Do you want to be with Menelaus or Paris? That's the problem. We women think that you don't even know what you want, yet you're willing to be involved in all this. Do you understand, Helen? If blood is spilled, and if it's even slightly your fault, then let it be spilled for something. As it is, we aren't willing to see our sons die for someone who doesn't seem to care."

How dare she insinuate that I don't care! Helen thought. "But I do care," she said through tears. "I care about all the sons of Troy. And the sons of Greece."

"Again, that's the problem!" Andromache said in a raised voice. "Choose your side. Troy or Greece? Paris or Menelaus?"

Helen didn't respond. Ever since she was a little girl, she hated hearing the truth. *That's why my relationship with Clytemnestra was so strained when we were young,* she realized. *Clytemnestra, like Andromache, can't resist telling everyone else the truth. I was born not even knowing the truth of who my father was—I had to hear the possible truths through rumor. I hate the truth.*

"You need to choose now," Andromache said. "Not one more moment may pass. The scouts have reported that a mighty Greek fleet has entered the waters of the Troad. They'll be here soon. You must tell me, now, before they arrive. Commit to something, or wallow in the loneliness of indecision."

Say something. As much as it hurts to accept something as truth, Andromache is right. I must make a choice and make it true.

"Fine," Helen replied. "I choose Paris. I won't look back. I choose Troy. Please tell the women that I choose Troy."

Suddenly, a loud and deep bell began to toll from above the courtyard. Helen and Andromache stared at each other. Then Andromache rose and started running toward the palace door. Helen ran after her. The two women sprinted across the great hall and ascended the spiral stone steps.

Priam was already standing on the parapet of the tower. The women joined him. They looked out, past the city, past the plains, past the beach, and into the Aegean. They saw hundreds of ships sailing toward the shore with Greek flags proudly waving. Helen grabbed the stone rail. Priam put his arm around her.

At the same time, on the Aegean close to Troy...

THE INITIAL BATTLE

ACHILLES STOOD ON the deck of his ship and looked to the towers and walls of Troy. It was the first time he'd ever seen them. *They're impressive,* he thought. *Agamemnon is wrong. There's no way this will end in a day.*

Next to him, he watched two Myrmidons throw a rope ladder off the side of the ship. Below on the water, he saw a small boat approach the side. Patroclus was on board. Achilles waved to him and watched Patroclus climb up the ladder.

"It's as we expected," Patroclus said as soon as he jumped onto the deck. "They've had a war council—all the commanders except for you were there—and they've decided to anchor the ships and wait until morning to attack the beach."

"And give Hector the entire night to prepare?" Achilles said.

"Their belief is that the sight of the ships will scare them enough to keep them inside the city. That way we can easily take the beach and the plain, then break through the gate and take the city."

"They still plan to do all this tomorrow? Without the element of surprise?"

"Yes, we'll sack the city and sail back to Greece within the week."

"If we wait until tomorrow," Achilles said, "the Trojans will slaughter us with arrows from their towers. We'll never take the beach, and we'll be living on ships for moons. No army has ever sustained itself living on ships. We must take the beach and the plain today so that we can make a proper camp. Why are they so focused on breaking the gate? It's impossible. We must build a base city of our own, then we can think about the gate."

"They all still firmly stand with Agamemnon. I believe they're clouded by the promise of returning in glory so quickly. Nobody wants to be the one to say that we might be here longer than a few moons."

"Clouded is never a way to fight a war. Standing in truth is the only path to victory."

"What do you intend to do?" Patroclus asked.

"I'm taking the Myrmidons to capture the beach. I don't care at all for Agamemnon's plan. We need a place to live."

"I agree," said Patroclus. "It makes the most sense. I'll get the men ready."

As the ships came nearer to the shore, Achilles began the process of communicating with the other Myrmidon vessels. He gave the order for the men to dress in full armor and prepare to storm the beach. The ships became a hive of activity with men doing what they had been well trained to do.

Achilles strapped on the magnificent armor that had been given to him by his father. It was made of thick bronze with gold accents that matched his hair. On his belt he attached a sword and made sure that two knives were held snugly in place on each leg.

"Patroclus," Achilles said, "it's time for you to sail to the main Myrmidon supply ship. Prepare the workers to set up the camp. Make sure to keep all the breeding animals far from the fighting. We don't want to risk losing any of them."

"Of course," Patroclus replied. "Don't worry. I'll have a Myrmidon camp all together before you can even begin to take off your armor."

"And, Patroclus …"

"I know, I know. No matter how much carnage I see, I'll wait until you say it's safe for the healers to approach any fallen man."

"Thank you."

Soon, they were close enough that the captains were worried about the ships hitting the bottom of the shore. The order was given to drop anchor. While the rest of the Greek fleet took their time, Achilles nodded to a Myrmidon commander. The commander climbed the mast of the ship with a torch and began to wave it in the air.

What are Agamemnon and the other kings thinking right now? Achilles wondered. *They must be furious. I know that none of them will thank me later when they have a place to camp, but they'll enjoy their fires and tents just the same as I.*

As silently as possible, Myrmidon soldiers climbed down the sides of their ships and slid into the water. Achilles did the same. The water was cold and filled in the space between armor and skin. However, they were so well trained that none were surprised by the temperature or the weight. *Slowly and surely, men, that's the way to go,* Achilles thought as he watched them. *Remember your training.*

They progressed, all fourteen thousand of them, until the leaders were able to stand on the ocean floor. This gave hope as those in front broke into a fast run. Achilles was almost halfway across the beach when he saw the first arrow fly from a Trojan tower. *We did it. A surprise!* he told himself. *We'll have no problem taking the beach.*

Thousands of arrows began to fly through the air. Achilles ignored the unlucky Myrmidons around him who fell. He kept running toward the plain. He could hear the thousands behind him. *I've passed the beach. Now across the plain and gain the land under my feet.*

Then, Achilles, with his eyes glued to the giant gate of Troy, saw the enormous doors slowly open. Standing in the center of the doorway, in full royal armor, was Hector. *Now, there's a presence I admire and want badly to end,* Achilles thought. Hector ran forward as hundreds of Trojans poured through the gate.

I wish I were on my chariot. It would make things faster, Achilles reflected, but he kept running. From the middle of the advancing Trojans, he saw another man emerge in royal armor. This man ran with a bow. *Not very smart to take a bow on the field. Why isn't he up in the tower?* The man rushed forward, passing even Hector, and took a stand before the rest of the Trojans. He threw off his helmet. *He must be Paris,* Achilles realized. *No one else could be that beautiful and that stupid.*

Paris strung his bow and fired an arrow directly at Achilles. *He must be desperate to be a hero,* Achilles thought as he dodged and grabbed the arrow with his hand as it flew by. Loud cries of praise erupted from the running Myrmidons. Achilles snapped the arrow in two, which made the praise even louder.

Hector stopped his charge to order Paris back. *At least Hector has some sense,* Achilles thought. The two sides finally clashed. Achilles grabbed his sword and began to fight his way across the plain. Thousands of Myrmidons kept pushing the Trojans back. Achilles had lost sight of Hector and looked desperately for him. He wanted to be the one to kill him.

It became clear that the mighty gate was working against the Trojans. Like a cork in a barrel of wine, it was keeping the massive forces of Troy inside while allowing just a few out at a time. The Trojans were outnumbered by the relentless Myrmidons.

"Achilles," a commander said as he ran up from behind, "we have the beach, and the plain is nearly ours. So fast!"

"Keep pushing," Achilles said. "Perhaps we can get to the gate and take all the area in front of the city. But keep watch for archers."

A loud horn blew from one of the towers. The Trojans stopped their charge and immediately ran back toward their city. *Retreat already?* Achilles thought. *They'll close the gate. Now Agamemnon will see that I was right. Now the long war begins.*

Achilles could see that it was fruitless to pursue. The few Trojans they would kill were not worth the risk of getting closer to the archers. He would not be able to reach the gates with a sizable-enough force. Achilles ordered the Myrmidon retreat.

He watched as Hector was the last Trojan standing in front of the open gates. Achilles waved to him and was not surprised that Hector waved back. *We'll meet another day,* he told himself. *Probably another year.*

Achilles walked slowly back to the shore. On the way, he saw Patroclus and his healers waiting in small boats just off the beach. Achilles signaled him, and the boats approached.

Myrmidons lay, either dead or wounded from arrows, on the plain. *Not that many*, Achilles noted. *We did good. Or, rather, the Trojan archers weren't prepared.*

"Achilles," said another commander, running up to him. "I just spoke with Hector himself—he rode out on horseback, and I was the first commander he came upon. He congratulates you on taking the beach and wants your permission to collect the Trojan dead for proper burial."

He's a well-trained and respectable soldier. I admire him, Achilles thought. "Yes," he said, "tell the Trojans that none of them will be harmed until every last one of their dead are removed."

Later that night, after bathing and eating, Achilles climbed a newly placed tent pole and surveyed the beach. The Myrmidon camp was almost complete, and he heard the sounds of reveling men through the dark. He also saw the makeshift funeral pyres that burned with respect for the Myrmidons who had died.

Achilles also noticed that the other Greek camps were beginning to take shape. *You're welcome, Agamemnon. You don't have to live on a ship for the next year. Not that you'll ever admit that you're grateful.*

Through the light of the moon, Achilles watched as the giant Trojan doors slowly closed.

After a long day and half the night, Patroclus finally returned to the tent. He was covered in sweat and other men's blood. Achilles helped him bathe and cooked a meal for him. They slept well.

Two moons later, in the Greek camp...

THE TEN-YEAR PLAN

KING NESTOR WAS old. Very old. Years earlier, he'd been one of the Argonauts—and he was old already then. Many told him to stay away from the war in Troy and rest. Initially, he agreed. But when he saw his son Antilochus preparing to command the forces, Nestor knew that he could never stay in Pylos. It wasn't that he didn't trust Antilochus, it was just that he didn't want to miss out on all the fun and excitement of battle. As it turned out, it was a good thing that he did come to Troy.

Over two moons had passed since the Myrmidons had taken the beach and the plain. Then the war seemed to stop. The Greeks built and perfected their camps while the Trojans stayed safely behind their walls.

Achilles still refused to speak with either Odysseus or Agamemnon. Nestor begged Agamemnon to visit Achilles and congratulate him on the first battle. But Agamemnon held firm to his resolve. Nestor became the only king Achilles would consult with. This was because Patroclus, whose father was also an Argonaut, was close to Nestor and praised him to Achilles.

Nestor had spent the last few days going between Achilles, Odysseus, and Agamemnon. *Achilles was right, we don't have the supplies to live here long,* Nestor thought. Achilles was the key to forming a plan of action. Without a plan, the Greeks would surely starve within another two moons. But since Agamemnon mistrusted anything that came from Achilles, Nestor mainly worked out the details by going constantly between Achilles and Odysseus.

Nestor knew that Odysseus had arranged a network of spies. With bribes and promises to Trojan servants, he'd been able to place several men inside the walls of Troy. *I would never want to fight a war against Odysseus,* Nestor thought. *That man is the only mortal alive capable of thinking like an Immortal.*

Nestor exited his tent and walked with Antilochus toward Agamemnon's tent. He felt it was time for a war council. Because of all Nestor's negotiations, Achilles agreed to join the council for the first time on Trojan soil.

Nestor saw Achilles walking toward him, just outside the Mycenae camp.

"Does Agamemnon know anything about our plan?" Achilles asked.

"A little," Nestor said. "Agamemnon is like a dog sometimes. You have to get him to follow you by throwing a scrap."

"He's like a dog more than just sometimes," Achilles said with a smirk.

"Please be civil," Nestor said.

They opened the tent flap and walked through. Odysseus, Diomedes, and Agamemnon were already sitting at the table. Nestor and Antilochus joined them. Then, to everyone's surprise, Achilles sat down at the table instead of taking his usual place apart from the others. Nestor kept his eyes on Agamemnon, but the king didn't betray any of his emotion at seeing Achilles.

They talked of mundane things while the other kings and commanders arrived. Then it was time to begin. *May the Immortals grant me the gift of speech,* Nestor thought. *This might be my last great act before I cross the river. But, then again, I might just outlive everyone in this tent.*

"Nestor has an idea," Agamemnon began. "It's been formed with the help of Odysseus and Achilles. Let's get this over with, Nestor."

Nestor stood and said, "Allow me to give the unpleasant news first. We now realize that this will be a long war. As Calchas had revealed from Athena, we won't step on Greek soil for another ten years."

Groans and murmurs penetrated the tent. The commanders shifted in their seats and shook their heads.

"From overnight to ten years?" Ajax the Greater said loudly. "How can this be?"

"What about supplies?" Ajax the Lesser said. "What will we eat?"

"Silence!" King Agamemnon shouted as he stood. "It's my fault. I underestimated the Trojan walls, and I'm deeply sorry for that. I take full responsibility. But my humility won't feed our men or forge new weapons. What's done, is done. Listen to Nestor for a way out of this."

"Yes," Nestor continued, "my old age has given me great wisdom. I urge you to forgive Agamemnon and praise his humble apology. The only way to victory is to accept a long war. Now, to answer your question, Greater Ajax, we now know that Troy can exist behind its walls for around ten years. Odysseus has gone to great lengths to learn of the situation inside the city. Odysseus, please tell us."

"There are two fresh wells in Troy," Odysseus said. "They have their own unending supply of drinkable water. There are massive granaries, both underground and above ground. They have stock pens and breeding groups of swine and birds. We also know that the hundreds of villages around the Troad are loyal. It's not unreasonable to believe that these people, who have lived their entire lives in this area, have ways of smuggling supplies into the city—even if we put up a blockade."

"But I have thought of a plan," said Nestor, "and Achilles has graciously agreed to comply. The Myrmidons will take one quarter of the men from each of our camps. They will form a roving army that Achilles will command. This army will attack and conquer the villages and city-states of the Troad. They'll send food and supplies back to us waiting here. They'll also send skilled men and women. The rest they will kill."

"However, those of you here won't be idle," Achilles said with a commanding voice. "Troy is now on the defensive. It's nearly impossible to win a war of walls while on the offensive. We'll change that and make them open the gates to attack us. For the next ten years, those of you staying here will build a giant wall of our own. The wall will protect the Greek camps from a Trojan attack. A deep trench will be dug in front of the wall. In order for the Trojans to get to us, they'll have to survive a trench and a wall."

"Our plan isn't hard to understand," Nestor said. "By conquering the villages, we'll replenish our supplies and, simultaneously, deplete Troy of theirs. They'll be forced to engage us, or starve. And when they do engage us, their task will be made difficult with a trench and a wall. Now, what do all of you say?"

"They'll say nothing," Agamemnon said forcefully. "This is our only option. Tonight we'll feast and drink the remainder of the wine. We must focus on improving the morale of the men. Spread the news of the plan. By giving the soldiers a task, we'll regain their trust. Achilles, I thank you and trust you. Leave as soon as possible, as we'll need the wine from the first village you sack."

That went well, Nestor thought. He congratulated Agamemnon and Achilles on their ability to work together. *I hope they'll continue, but they probably won't. I'm old enough to know this.*

Five years later, across the Troad…

AT LYRNESSUS

IT HAD NEVER occurred to Patroclus that the world could be any different than it was. When at war, armies killed each other and took the spoils as they saw fit. People were enslaved. As kind-hearted as he was, the reality of war seemed as normal to him as eating. There was never even an inkling in his mind that there were other ways for a culture to operate.

Over five years had passed since the last time Patroclus had seen Odysseus, Agamemnon, or any of the Greeks who stayed behind at Troy. In that time he'd seen the traveling Greek army, commanded by Achilles, annihilate villages and entire city-states. He and his healers worked to help the wounded of the Greek army. He saw a lot of pain and death, followed by long periods of living on spoils taken from the sacked people.

A constant caravan operated between the army of Achilles and the beach at Troy. Food, supplies, treasure, and people were transported weekly. They heard news, in the form of messengers from Nestor, that told of the Greeks' progress in building their own wall. Sometimes, Odysseus would send congratulations for a victory over whatever village had recently been sacked. They never heard anything from, or about, Agamemnon.

Many of their new slaves had been slaves well before there was a war. These were often skilled people who cared little about whom they worked for. Patroclus and Achilles knew that they could win their loyalty by making their lives just a little better than they had been before their city was taken. This philosophy worked well in the traveling army camp. Patroclus had no idea if the Greeks at Troy treated their new slaves using the same principle. He sometimes wondered about it.

Every once in a while, someone from the ruling class was captured. These people were more difficult to deal with. It was up to Achilles and Patroclus to deal with those in this situation. Most of these privileged men were killed; a few who demonstrated a genuine willingness to cooperate were spared. The women from these higher classes usually killed themselves within a few days of capture. Those who didn't were put to use as concubines. Often, these women, too, eventually killed themselves.

It had been a week since Achilles and the traveling army sacked the city-state of Lyrnessus. Patroclus was exhausted. *The first week after conquest is always the worst,* he thought. *Now that everyone has either been healed or has died, it's time to sleep.*

He was alone in the tent. He bathed and put on a newly washed tunic. Patroclus liked this time of the evening. He felt clean and had time to relax before Achilles returned from the day's work. He enjoyed listening to the sounds of the camp around him. *Even in this situation, people are living,* he reflected. He sat on a chair and drank some wine just brought from the former palace of Lyrnessus.

Two women entered the tent, followed by Achilles. Patroclus was surprised, as all of their personal servants had, so far, been men. The women had been washed and were wearing clean, simple tunics. Their hair was combed. Both had an exotic look, but one was much taller than the other. As was his custom, Patroclus scanned their arms and faces for any sign of wounds. *I wonder if I'll ever cease this habit? Probably not, there will never be a world without war.*

"We have to talk about these," Achilles said. "I was walking past the women's tents and noticed that these two were assisting with the birth of a child. I thought maybe you could use them."

Patroclus stood and said, "Hello, my name is Patroclus."

Achilles said to the women with a laugh, "You'll find that Patroclus is a much better person than I am."

"What are your names?" Patroclus asked.

The shorter one answered, "I'm Briseis. This is Chryseis."

Her voice sounds defiant, Patroclus thought. *She must be of royal birth.* "Are both of you from the royal family of Lyrnessus?" he asked.

Briseis looked surprised then said, "Just me. Chryseis is a priestess."

Achilles said, "A priestess for which Immortal?"

"Apollo," Chryseis replied.

Achilles made a small moan and looked at Patroclus. Patroclus just raised an eyebrow and continued questioning the women. "It's odd that either of you know about childbirth." he said. "Both of you have a station above midwife."

Briseis answered, "I'm the daughter of a midwife. My father was proficient in the art of healing wounds. A prince of Lyrnessus noticed me when I assisted with the birth of his niece. He took to me and we married. I wasn't always a princess."

"And you?" Patroclus said, looking toward Chryseis.

"I just happened to be nearby when Briseis started to help the birthing woman," Chryseis said. "I helped and did what she asked, but I have no training."

"Apollo doesn't care for the Greeks," Achilles said. "The priestess needs to go. She has nothing to offer us that would make Apollo's wrath worth it."

Patroclus watched as Chryseis's face filled with terror. *I don't feel right killing her*, Patroclus thought. "This woman was noticed simply because she wanted to help," he said. "I don't believe that it's fair to execute her."

After a moment, Achilles said, "Agreed. We'll send her back to the other Greeks at Troy."

"But I want to keep the shorter one, Briseis, here," Patroclus said. "We need healers, and perhaps she's learned things that we don't know."

Achilles grabbed Chryseis softly by the arm and led her to the tent opening. He left Briseis standing in the middle of the tent.

Before they exited, Briseis said, "Can you tell me what happened to the baby? I think I'm owed that after all my work."

Achilles stopped, paused, did not face them, and said, "This is war."

Patroclus noticed that Briseis was visibly upset at this comment. He chose to ignore thoughts about the baby and began to fix some food for the woman.

Two years later...

INSIDE TROY

ECTOR RAN ACROSS the great hall and took the spiral steps two at a time. But when he saw the sunlight at the end of the stairs, he suddenly stopped. He thought, *What am I in such a hurry for? Father is certainly not.* He took a few deep breaths, finished the steps, and walked out onto the parapet. Priam was standing alone, as he often did, looking over the Greek camp and toward the Aegean.

Hector hadn't been up on the highest parapet for over a year. As he approached his father, he looked at the wall that the Greeks had built. *It's so much taller than the last time I saw it. What a mistake! We no longer have the upper hand.*

"Father," Hector said, "I bring news."

"Good news of your child, I hope," Priam answered. "I heard that Andromache's pains began during the night."

"Yes, Father, and it's wonderful news. My son, Astyanax, has been born. He's healthy and Andromache is fine. I've already held him—the future king of Troy—with my own hands."

"Praise the Immortals! Has the priest of Apollo been here?"

"Yes, Father, and nothing to worry about. There was no prophesy."

Priam breathed deeply, embraced Hector, and said, "This is, indeed, wonderful news. We need wonderful news. I'll send the word out through all the messengers. Tonight, we'll celebrate in the city of Troy."

Say it or not? Hector wondered. *Should I start a fight on this day of all days? Yes, I owe it to Astyanax and his future.* "Father," Hector said, "how can we celebrate? There's hardly any wine left in storage, and the granaries began the strictest rationing over six moons ago. The people will hate us if we celebrate."

"Don't start with me again, Hector," Priam said.

"How can I not? Is Astyanax to be the first king of Troy who has never ever been outside the walls of the city? What kind of life would that be for him? What kind of life is it for any of us?"

"The Greeks will leave any day now. You'll see. This is how it's always been. My father and his father before him defended Troy by locking the gate. Our walls have never been breached, and the enemy always tires. This time is no different."

"Father, open your eyes! Look at that wall. This is a different enemy—much smarter than the enemies of old. Achilles has attacked most every city of the Troad. He wins, easily, every time. There's no shortage of supplies going to the Greek army on the beach. And, even worse, our friends now hate us because we've done nothing but sit behind our walls. We've let them suffer and die for our safety. More than seven years, now, Father! Years!"

"I've heard all this before," Priam said. "You know my dedication to my ancestors and to the Immortals."

"Your ancestors are dead," Hector said. "It's time to think of your grandson and his legacy. Will there be anything left of Troy? The Greeks control the Hellespont and profit from our tariffs. The Trojan treasury is low."

"Hector, I understand all this. You're a warrior—the greatest Trojan hero—and you're anxious to fight. I'm older and much more experienced. I've survived wars and battles, more than I care to remember. Patience is what's required."

"Patience isn't a virtue that knows about Achilles. Father, he and his ruthless army are still on the other side of the Troad. But there are reports that they're moving back to our beach. Right now, the Greek forces we face at our gate are only half their number. We need to attack now, before Achilles returns."

"You may think that you know all, Hector," said Priam. "But I have eyes and ears everywhere. This has been my country longer than it has been yours. Despite what you think, I know how to fight a battle without swords. My sources tell me that things are bad in the Greek camp. Agamemnon can't maintain control now that the wall and trench are complete. The Greeks have nothing to do, and that restlessness leads to trouble. They drink the wine that Achilles sends. They gamble and argue amongst themselves. Fights break out throughout the day and night. I've been told that Agamemnon is at his wit's end and that the Greeks will sail before Achilles returns."

"But, Father," Hector begged, "just think about—"

"Stop this," came a voice from the stairs. Hector turned and saw Paris walking onto the parapet.

"How long have you been there?" Priam asked.

"The whole time," Paris answered. "I've heard everything."

"I'm glad that you have," said Priam. "Hector, I can see that you and I will never agree. Perhaps it's time to add a third vote—perhaps Apollo sent Paris to us at this very moment. Paris, you heard everything. What is your opinion? Do we stay within the city, or open the gate and fight?"

"I came to tell you that I've made my own decision," Paris said. "And it's neither of yours. I'll challenge Menelaus to a duel over Helen. This is the way it has been for hundreds of years. We should have offered it as soon as the Greeks arrived, but I was ignorant then."

"No, Paris," Priam said. "Things aren't done this way any longer."

Hector said, "Paris, you—"

"Stop!" Paris interrupted. "Both of you. Just stop. I've already sent the messenger to Menelaus, and he has accepted, with Agamemnon's approval. If I win, the Greeks will leave and Helen will stay. But if I die, the Greeks will leave with Helen. Either way, the two of you will have your city back to prepare for the new Prince Astyanax."

Paris surprises me with this boldness, Hector thought. *I wonder how the duel will go. Paris is younger and has more stamina than Menelaus, but he's only good with a bow. Either way, what do I care? Andromache and my son wait for me.*

A few days later…

THE DUEL

Paris wore the royal armor of a prince of Troy. In the sunlight, the gold accents glimmered off his helmet and breastplate. He had a sword hanging on his belt and an extra dagger strapped to his leg. He carried a heavy Trojan shield. *It feels odd not to have my bow,* he thought.

One side of the giant gate was opened just enough to let Paris through. He took a deep breath and passed through to the other side. *This is the first time I've been out of Troy for years. I would love to run to the water. Maybe I can finish this quick and do just that.*

When he was outside the wall, he turned and looked up. He couldn't see the palace parapet from this vantage point. But he knew that Helen and Priam were standing on it and would be able to see him when he moved farther from the wall. As he turned, he saw Hector standing on top of the wall itself, above the gates. Hector bowed to him, and he bowed back.

Finally, he turned to face the Greeks. He was startled to see how many of them were waiting in long lines to see the duel. *They're so quiet,* he thought. *There must be a thousand men here, and all you can hear is an occasional* horse. *They aren't dressed for battle—it's good that they intend to honor the agreement of the duel.*

Standing in front of the Greek lines were two men: Menelaus and Agamemnon. *I wish Hector had come with me,* Paris thought. Menelaus wore his armor, and Agamemnon wore a long tunic, like all the other Greeks. Menelaus appeared larger than Paris had imagined. *I have to remember what Hector told me,* Paris told himself. *He's older and not as swift. I need to make him tired and then go in for the kill.*

As Paris approached, Agamemnon stepped back against his men. There wouldn't be any pomp and circumstance to begin the fight—everything had been decided by the agreement. Menelaus stepped forward.

Paris wasted no time. *I need to show him that I'm in charge.* He ran toward Menelaus, retrieving his sword and coming at him with a wide swipe of the blade. Menelaus stepped back. Paris's sword had nothing to hit, and the force of the swing caused him to lose his balance. He nearly fell as loud laughter erupted from the Greeks.

Paris was embarrassed and did not look toward Troy. He knew that many eyes were on him from the tops of the walls and towers. He regained his balance and ran toward Menelaus. But just as he was within reach, he switched direction and backed away. He repeated this action three more times. Menelaus just stood there. *Why isn't he coming for me?* Paris wondered.

During his fourth charge, Paris caught a glimpse of Agamemnon. He had a smirk on his face that Paris hated. It gave him energy, and he lifted his sword, making a strike toward Menelaus. For the first time in the duel, Menelaus had underestimated Paris. The sword made contact with the older man's left arm and clanked loudly on the armor. Menelaus fell back.

Without wasting any time, Menelaus threw his shield to the ground, withdrew his sword, and came at Paris with a fierce thrashing motion. His first blow landed on Paris's shield. Paris felt the harsh vibrations throughout his entire body. He was glad when the vibrations stopped, but then he noticed that Menelaus was striking again. Paris held on to the shield with all his might, but the force of each blow shattered the strength of his hand. Knowing he would soon drop his shield, Paris dropped to the ground and covered his head with the shield. Several more blows followed.

When Menelaus finally backed away, the Greek forces once again laughed. Menelaus bowed to the crowd and turned back to face Paris. *Why didn't he kill me when I was down?* Paris wondered. *He must want to humiliate me.*

Paris got up from the ground and switched the shield to his other hand. He knew it wasn't smart to move his sword to his nondominant side, but he had no choice due to his loss of strength. *Make him tired,* he told himself.

Paris, once again, began the dance of advancing and retreating. However, Menelaus would not engage. He simply stood there. After several advances, Paris soon discovered that he himself was the one who was getting tired. His shield felt excruciatingly heavy. He grew afraid that the look on his face was betraying his weakness.

Suddenly, Menelaus sprang at him with one giant leap. Menelaus's sword easily disarmed Paris by sending his sword flying through the air. Then, with a great kick from his metal boots, Menelaus kicked the shield from Paris's grasp. Paris was defenseless.

Menelaus threw his own sword down on the ground. He smacked Paris on the side of his head with his fist. Paris's helmet flew from his head. Menelaus hit him again. And again. Paris fell to the ground.

Menelaus let loose with all the fury of a man who believed he'd lost his wife. His feet and fists were relentless. Paris heard huge cheers coming from the Greek soldiers. He started to taste blood. His eyesight was clouded with tears and more blood. He tried to cover his head with his hands, but the blows still came. *Make it stop! Make it stop! Aphrodite, make it stop!*

Then the blows stopped.

"You have no business here, Hector," Menelaus said. "Go back inside your prison."

Paris struggled to lift his head and was able to see that Hector was walking toward him. He felt Hector's massive arms lift him to his feet. He was still having trouble seeing, and he leaned heavily on his brother.

"This wasn't a fair duel," Hector said. "The sun is intense this morning. From my perch on the wall I could see the reflection of armor under your Greek tunic. You came prepared for a battle. You were never going to honor the duel, no matter who won."

"That is a lie," said Agamemnon, stepping forward and joining his own brother. "It's a Trojan lie."

"Then strip off your tunic and show me," Hector replied.

"We don't take orders from you," Agamemnon retorted.

Paris and Hector limped their way toward the gate. Paris didn't know if Menelaus or Agamemnon was following them.

"Coward!" Menelaus shouted. "Coward! Stay and fight like a man!"

Now all the Greeks started shouting insults at the Trojan brothers. Then Paris passed out.

He woke sometime later in his own bed. It was dark outside. He was in immense pain. Someone had cleaned him and put him in the bed. *Was it Helen?* he wondered. *Did she care for me? Funny, this is the first time I thought about her all day, even though I was almost killed for her honor. What happened at the gate? Where's Hector?*

Paris opened his eyes and saw a young nurse sitting on a chair next to him. The nurse smiled at him, then waved her hand over his body. Immediately, he felt his pain go away. He felt relief so quickly that he sat up and looked carefully at the nurse. *This is no nurse who cares for me.*

"Aphrodite," Paris said, "you heard my prayer and came to my aid."

"Yes," she answered, "for your time has not yet come."

"Where's Helen? Does she care? Did I embarrass her?"

Aphrodite motioned with her hand. Paris looked to the other side of the bed and saw Helen sitting there. *Still,* he thought, *the most beautiful woman in the world.*

"She was embarrassed," Aphrodite said. "But she now understands that you were never meant for such displays of strength."

"Paris," Helen said, "I'm so sorry. I should never have been silent when I heard you intended to fight Menelaus. I'm here now."

Helen began to cry and dropped her head on Paris's chest. He put his hands on her head. Aphrodite stood.

"What happened at the gate?" Paris asked.

"The Greeks refused to show if they were prepared for battle," Helen said through tears. "They didn't dare betray themselves, and they retreated. There wasn't any fighting and the gate has closed."

"The Immortals grow tired of this war," Aphrodite said abruptly. "Enough is enough. I've decided that it's time for

Troy to attack the Greeks and end this. There can be no more hiding behind the walls."

"My father won't hear of it," Paris said. "Hector can't convince him. How can we get him to order an attack?"

Aphrodite continued, "I had a great love affair with Priam's cousin, Prince Anchises of Dardania. We have a child together, my son Aeneas. Priam respects Aeneas. I have sent for Aeneas, and he always obeys me. Aeneas and Hector, working together, will change Priam's mind. I'll see to it."

"Aphrodite," Helen said, "how can we call for you when we need you?"

But by the time she finished speaking, both of them noticed that the woman was no longer there. Helen moved closer and draped herself over Paris.

It's very good to have an Immortal on your side, he thought. *Especially when you're in pain.*

One year later, back with Achilles and his army
somewhere in the Troad...

A SMALL FAMILY

I T HAD BEEN three years since Briseis watched as Greeks killed her husband and sacked her entire city. But in that time she became almost as indispensable to Achilles and Patroclus as they were to each other.

She lived and worked with them. At first, she'd often hear the other soldiers talk about her and wonder how she had such unlimited access to Achilles. Since everyone knew that Achilles preferred Patroclus, she heard the men ponder what she could possibly offer him. Then, as the moons passed, it became evident to the entire roving camp that Briseis was as smart as she was diligent.

Since an early age, Briseis had been devoted to the art of healing. When she wasn't working with her parents, she was bothering other healers to share their knowledge. Her skills were superior to those of Patroclus. *He's the most interesting man,* Briseis thought. *Patroclus isn't bothered when I can do something that he can't. He watches me and then asks me about it. There's surely no other man like him alive. It's too bad that someone like him isn't Immortal. Perhaps we'd all be better off if those with power acted as Patroclus does.*

However, as much as she learned from Patroclus, she learned more about humanity from Achilles. At first, this was shocking. *How can this ruthless killer come back to the tent, wash, and be the second-most wonderful human I've ever met?* she wondered. *He recites poetry better than any bard and has a surprising wit.* Then, as she grew to accept him, she began to wonder what it must be like to have to kill, or to have to watch everyone you care for be killed. *Achilles has to make that decision every day.*

There hadn't been any fighting for over three moons. This meant that each day, her daily routine of checking on wounds was getting easier and easier. Most of the wounded had either healed or died. She finished cleaning and wrapping one of the last who still suffered, then looked around for Patroclus. She saw him sitting on the ground and leaning against a tent pole. *He must have finished before me. It's nice to see him relaxing.*

She walked to him and sat. He scooted over to make room for her to share the pole.

"How's the last one?" Patroclus asked. "The soldier you were just checking on."

"No change," she replied. "It still festers, but the wound has not corrupted the skin around it. It's difficult to know what to do. How long can he live with the pain?"

"There was that soldier we treated when we camped at Mount Ida. Remember? His wound festered for several moons and did, eventually, heal."

"That might happen in this case, too. But this man seems to be in greater pain, or maybe he has a lower threshold. I think in five days, if we don't see any improvement, we should ask him if he wants to live in pain or not."

"That seems wise," Patroclus said.

"But I interrupted you," Briseis said. "What were you thinking about?"

"What would you do if you could do anything?"

"You mean, if I were still in Lyrnessus married to Mynes? I suppose I'd be weaving some sort of tapestry with the other royal women."

"No, not what would you be doing if we'd never met. What would you want to do if you had freedom, time, and the riches to do whatever you wanted?"

"Are you worried that I don't feel free? Are you concerned that I resent being a slave?"

"I don't ever think about you as a slave," Patroclus said. "You're free to do whatever you want, even run away if you like. Achilles and I would never pursue you. I hope you know that."

"I know that," Briseis said. "But I'm smart enough to know that I'm attached to the two of you. Not because I have to be, but because I want to be. Mynes was a nice husband, but there was nothing particularly interesting about him. We never talked really about anything. And, I'm sure you can imagine that other women think I'm a bit odd."

"I often feel the same way around men."

They chuckled and leaned against each other. Briseis sighed and sank into the folds of the tent. She had learned from Patroclus to revel in the fading sunlight and submit to relaxation.

"I guess," Briseis said, "if I could go anywhere, I'd want to go to Egypt. The healers there are far superior to us. They know things about what occurs inside the body. I want to learn from them."

"The Egyptians have been cutting into bodies forever," Patroclus said. "They preserve people. It's odd. But they probably have gained a lot of knowledge from seeing the inside. Perhaps when all this is done we can go there together."

"You would leave Achilles? I can't believe that."

"Of course not. He would have to come with us. He'll be famous when this war ends—when he becomes the hero who conquered the famous walls of Troy. Achilles won't have a problem finding soldiers to command in Egypt."

"Your bond is strong."

"I can't explain it. I don't know that anyone can, except perhaps his mother, Thetis. She seems to know us better than we know ourselves."

"She's an Immortal. They always know a lot and share a little." *I forgot*, Briseis thought. *He doesn't like it when I criticize the Immortals.*

"Thetis says that together we're the most complete human ever alive," Patroclus said. "Between the two of us, we hold the combined compassion, wrath, intelligence, and physical strength of an entire village. That's what she says, anyway. But I think that the two of us just like to be with each other. That's all. It's the enjoyment we have of each other that brings out the best in us."

"Well," said Briseis, "here comes the other half of the combined human now."

Achilles was riding across the field on a horse. He waved to them and turned the horse in their direction.

"It looks like he was just out for a pleasure ride," Patroclus said. "It's nice to see him do something like that."

Achilles stopped the horse and jumped off in a single motion. He sat down next to Patroclus and tried to lean against the tent pole. But the weight was too great and the tent started to dip. The three sat straighter.

"I have news," Achilles said. "News that I think you'll like. We're packing up tomorrow to begin our journey back to Troy."

"It's finally time?" Patroclus asked.

"Yes. Odysseus sent word that things are bad inside Troy. We'll return and unite the Greek army. The Trojans will have to open the gate and engage us. They can't exist any longer in isolation."

My time with Patroclus and Achilles has taught me that I can believe in anything, Briseis thought. *Maybe we can finish the war and travel together to Egypt. Anything is possible.*

One moon later, in the Greek camp...

A BIG PROBLEM

"ODYSSEUS," A SOLDIER said, "the scouts report that they're in sight."

"Thank you," he replied.

Odysseus strapped on his sandals, left the tent, and mounted his horse. He rode through the Greek camps and out onto the plain alongside Troy. Before long, he saw the first lines of the traveling army, being led by Achilles on his chariot. *Achilles looks stronger now than when he left all those years ago*, Odysseus thought.

He stopped his horse and waved to Achilles. Achilles sped up, breaking away from his army, and met Odysseus.

"It's been a long time," Odysseus said.

"But a productive time," Achilles answered.

"I know. You've supplied us well. No matter how this war ends, I think that Nestor's ten-year plan will live on as the defining moment of victory."

"Is Nestor still alive?"

"Of course," Odysseus said. "I think he's ten years younger now. His son looks his same age."

"What about the wall?" Achilles asked.

"It's complete. And the trench as well. You'll see it when you come around. But I rode out to tell you that there won't be much help from our army in getting your army settled. There won't be a welcoming contingent or any sort of celebration tonight."

"Why? Is Agamemnon still angry? I thought that after all this time he'd finally—"

"No," Odysseus answered. "There's a plague among the soldiers. Many are weak."

"Plagues are the work of Apollo. What did Agamemnon do to insult the Immortal?"

"Calchas is working on it. He will commune with the Immortals and discover Agamemnon's offense."

"Calchas is still alive?" Achilles asked.

"Like I said, you did an excellent job keeping us supplied. Calchas has been well fed and cared for in his old age. Come. Agamemnon wants to speak with you in his tent. He's not been stricken with the plague."

Achilles rode back to his men and spoke with Patroclus. Odysseus waved to Patroclus as Achilles returned to Odysseus. Then the two of them sped off toward the Greek camp, Achilles on chariot and Odysseus on horseback. They crossed the deeply dug Greek trench on a small wooden bridge that led to an opening in the wall.

I think Achilles actually looks impressed with our work! Odysseus thought. After they entered, he maneuvered his horse around groups of visibly sick men. Eventually, they arrived at Agamemnon's tent.

Agamemnon sat at his table with Menelaus, Nestor, Diomedes, and Ajax the Greater. Odysseus noticed that Calchas was sitting on a chair in a dark corner of the tent. *There's tension in here,* he thought. *Something has happened. At the moment of Achilles's return—what bad timing! That priest has caused some sort of turmoil again, no doubt.*

Nestor rose and embraced Achilles. He offered his congratulations and gave Achilles his seat at the table.

"Achilles," Agamemnon said, "welcome. I thank you for your work. We've been well supplied and, as you can see, we've been able to complete the wall. However, unfortunately, we won't be able to offer a feast of celebration. I'm sure Odysseus told you that we're in the midst of a plague. Many are too sick to even stand."

"How long has this been going on?" Achilles asked.

"For a moon," Nestor replied. "I've never seen a plague this bad before. Pretty much all of the common soldiers have it. We've—"

"We've consulted the person who's supposed to take care of it," Agamemnon interrupted. "But Calchas here hasn't been able to discover a remedy with Apollo."

"As I said, King Agamemnon," Calchas replied in a calm voice, "Immortal Apollo is angry and wants us to figure out how we offended him. I need time."

As they spoke, Menelaus waved to a soldier and asked that refreshments be brought for Achilles. Three women entered the tent with wine, bread, and strips of cooked meat. Odysseus watched them set the food on the table and noticed that Achilles stared strangely at one of the women. *I wonder what that's all about,* he mused.

"Calchas," Agamemnon said, "you've run out of time. We need this plague solved, now! The Trojans have spies among us. We know this. They'll find out that we're incapacitated. We know that Aeneas is coming near with his Dardanian army. If Troy attacks us while we're this weak, we'll lose everything we've worked for."

As Agamemnon and Calchas argued, Odysseus began to pay attention to a side conversation. Achilles had turned around to address the woman he was staring at.

"You look familiar," Achilles said. "How do I know you?"

"You captured me at Lyrnessus," the woman replied.

"Lyrnessus?" Achilles asked. "You were with Briseis, I remember. You helped her with a birth. You're a priestess of Apollo, right?"

As soon as he mentioned the woman's former role, the tent grew silent. *This might be the information we've been waiting for*, Odysseus thought.

"This is my new concubine," Agamemnon said.

"New?" Achilles replied. "It's been years since we sacked Lyrnessus."

Odysseus said, "She was part of a group that was apprehended by the Lycian army. They kept her, and the rest of the spoils of Lyrnessus, for years until we attacked and got them all back. She just came here lately."

"Girl," Agamemnon said, "what's your name? And how long have you been here?"

"I'm Chryseis. I've been in your tent for a moon, perhaps longer."

"And," Calchas interjected, "you were a priestess of Apollo?"

"Yes."

"Well," Calchas continued, "there's our answer. We've offended Apollo by defiling his priestess. Return this girl and allow her to find the Lyrnessian refugees. Then, the plague will end."

Most in the room gave a sigh of relief. *This seems simple enough to fix*, Odysseus thought. *The men will be strong again by morning.*

"No," Agamemnon said.

"What do you mean?" Odysseus asked. "The situation is clear. She must go back."

"She stays here," Agamemnon said.

"You have plenty of concubines," Diomedes said. "Send her back and end this plague."

"It's not about her being a concubine," Agamemnon said. "She was captured by Achilles and given to me to honor my position. If I give her away, I'll be losing the honor that Achilles granted me."

"I've sent you many spoils," Achilles said.

"And I want them all," Agamemnon replied. "The men already think that I'm weak. We had a disastrous duel between Menelaus and Paris. The men wanted me to order an attack, but I was hesitant. Then the plague. The men think I'm faulty. If I give up the part of my honor that lives with this woman, they'll lose faith in me."

"What about this other girl?" Odysseus said. "Achilles, you mentioned that this Chryseis was captured with another. You called her Briseis."

"Yes," Achilles said. "What does that have to do with anything?"

"It solves our situation," Odysseus said. "Agamemnon will send Chryseis back to Apollo. You'll give him Briseis as a replacement for his honor. This way Apollo is pacified and Agamemnon still gets honor from you. Simple."

"Never!" Achilles shouted. "Briseis is mine."

Odysseus noticed that Agamemnon called a soldier, whispered into his ear, then looked at Achilles. *Something isn't as it seems*, Odysseus thought.

"What can you want with a concubine anyway, Achilles?" Nestor asked. "Was Patroclus lost?"

"Patroclus is fine," Achilles answered. "I'm thinking of him right now as much as I'm thinking of myself. Briseis knows the art of healing. She's most useful to us, especially Patroclus, with the wounded soldiers. The entire Myrmidon camp would be saddened if she left us."

"Nonsense," Agamemnon said. "She's a woman—a concubine, no less. I imagine that Patroclus enjoys gossiping with her, as women do. Healing? Unlikely. And what if it's true? We haven't had Patroclus and his healers here for all these years. We need a few healers for the leaders, and that's it. If a soldier gets wounded, we just kill him. What do we need more healers like Patroclus and this other woman for?"

Achilles jumped to his feet. "Do not insult Patroclus! I don't need a sword to rip your head off your body. You know I can do it, and I will!"

"My apologies," Agamemnon said quickly and remorsefully. "Really, I do sincerely apologize. Patroclus is a better man than anyone in this tent. But Odysseus has offered the perfect solution."

Then the tent flap opened and a soldier ushered in Briseis. Odysseus watched as she made eye contact with Achilles. *She thinks of herself as his equal*, Odysseus realized. *Just as Patroclus does. Achilles speaks the truth. She must be wise in the ways of healing, or she would never have such confidence. But the plague must end, or we'll all perish. Is there another way?*

Agamemnon stood and walked toward the tent opening. Odysseus also stood and put his hand softly on Achilles's chest.

"Send the woman Chryseis back to Apollo," Agamemnon said. "Bring the girl Briseis to join my other concubines."

Agamemnon left the tent. Achilles pushed Odysseus aside and started to follow. But Menelaus and Diomedes quickly stood, ran to him, and grabbed his arms. *There's no way those two can restrain him. None of us can*, Odysseus thought.

"Achilles," Odysseus said, "please stop. Apollo is an Immortal. Even you can't fight him."

"Agamemnon is mortal," Achilles said. "I can fight him and kill to win."

"Even though he's not Immortal, Agamemnon is still more than a mortal," Odysseus said. "He represents Greece. Whether you like it or not, the men see him as the commander of commanders. You know this is true, and there's nothing that any of us can do about it. The Mycenae soldiers are loyal. As are the Spartans."

"Then," Achilles began, "I won't be Greek any longer. I appealed to the decency of you all by explaining how important Briseis is to me and Patroclus. But you wouldn't listen. I'm ashamed to be Greek. From this moment, the Myrmidons won't fight. You're all on your own. I'll drink wine and watch as the Trojans conquer the Greeks."

"Achilles," Nestor said, "you must listen to reason."

"There is no reason here!" Achilles shouted. "I gave you the reason why this woman was important to me, and all of you allowed Agamemnon to take her. Whatever happens to you Greeks, you all deserve it."

Achilles left and Odysseus went after him. He wanted to stop Achilles and try, one more time, to speak with him. However, Odysseus suddenly saw a group of soldiers get up off the ground and start to stretch. He listened as they talked about feeling better and getting something to eat. *The plague is over already*, he thought. *We'll just have to accept that for now.*

He let Achilles continue, alone, back to the Myrmidon camp.

A few days later...

THE FIRST TROJAN OFFENSIVE

THERE WASN'T A horse alive that Hector couldn't ride. His nickname had been Horse Tamer for most of his life. He was the finest horseman in Troy, which is saying a lot for a city so revered for its horsemen. After all, the horse was the symbol of Troy and was depicted on the breastplate of most Trojan soldiers.

Hector stood in the courtyard of the palace wearing his full royal armor. He inspected the armor on his favorite horse. *Today is finally the day, after all these long years,* he thought. *Thanks to Aeneas, today we'll take back our freedom.*

The other, nonfighting members of the royal family, including Helen, came into the courtyard. Andromache approached carrying the infant Astyanax. Hector kissed him on the forehead.

"May we leave him a great city to rule," Hector said.

"May you, Hector, return to rule after Priam. I pray that no generation is skipped," his wife said.

"Don't be afraid. I'm not."

"You must come back to me," Andromache said. "I can't live without you."

"Don't let that thought cross your mind," Hector replied. "The Greeks will flee on their ships, and I'll be back by midday."

Whether or not I return alive isn't as important as Troy winning this war, he thought. *Andromache and Astyanax must not become slaves. I could never rest in death if they were.*

"The plan is strong," Hector said. "Our spies tell us that Achilles and Agamemnon are fighting with each other. The Myrmidons won't raise arms against us. We also have surprise on our side, and Aeneas is approaching. Our timing is perfect."

"I'll be in the temple the entire day while you're away," Andromache said. "I won't stop praising the Immortals until you're safe."

Hector kissed her lovingly on the mouth and checked that he had his sword and dagger. He jumped onto his horse and looked up to the palace parapet. He raised his hand toward Priam and watched his father return the gesture.

Horses carrying the other princes, including Paris, entered the courtyard from the royal stables. Hector gave a whistle, and the entire group galloped out and into the city.

As they raced down the city streets, lower and lower around the spiral, the people came to their windows and doors. They had been told to be silent, so as not to alert the Greeks, and they waved various clothes and rags in support. As the soldiers neared the bottom layer of the city, Hector heard the groaning sound of the massive gates being fully opened for the first time in years. He sped up.

We timed it perfectly, he thought. They reached the gate just as it opened completely. Thousands of Trojan foot soldiers waited and let the horses pass. Now the entire mass of Trojan forces raced toward the Greeks.

But as they reached the trench, lines of Greek soldiers popped up with spears. *They know! It's not a surprise,* Hector realized as he steered his horse around several spears and entered the trench. However, the grade and the spears were too much, and Hector felt his horse fall away from him. Before he knew it, he was off his horse and on his feet. Many other Trojans met the same fate and were attempting to free themselves from dying horses.

The Greeks retrieved their swords from their belts and attacked.

This doesn't look good, Hector thought. *We can't retreat this early. It would mean the end of Troy.* "Fight! Do not give!" he yelled. "Get to their wall! Think of your city!"

The Trojan soldiers kept piling into the trench. It was a mass of men. Blood flowed fast from wounds on both sides. There was so much blood that it was beginning to be difficult for Hector to tell the Trojans apart from the Greeks. Everyone, and every piece of armor, looked red.

We're being slaughtered in here, he thought in despair.

Then Hector heard the shouts of a large group of men. He turned around and saw that Aeneas had arrived with his Dardanian army. The Dardanians, because they weren't living behind a wall, had more access to supplies than the Trojans did. Hector watched in awe and gratitude as chariots arrived with large wooden planks. The Dardanians were well trained, and they quickly flung the planks across the trench. This made it possible for Hector, and thousands of Trojan soldiers, to climb out of the trench and attack from above.

The tides had turned. Hector kept pushing his forces forward. *Yes!* he thought. *They're starting to run back inside their makeshift Greek wall.*

Other Trojans must have noticed because new energy sprang from their midsts. There is a point in every battle when one side knows it must retreat. Hector smiled when he saw that the Greeks had come to this realization. A signal was given from the top of the wall, and the Greeks, as fast as they could, hurled themselves backward and through various openings. Then the openings were sealed with stone.

The Trojans and their allies shouted with the full energy of victory, "We've taken their trench and pushed them back inside their own camp!"

It took the rest of the day for Hector to organize the army. He needed to make sure that they would hold the Greek trench while they rested and prepared for the next day's battle. *The next battle is for the wall itself,* he told himself.

In the evening, Hector and his royal brothers rode back into the city on fresh horses. They were met with cheers coming from every window and door in Troy. There were so many people shouting "Hector!" at one time that nobody could hear anything else. *The Greeks must be able to hear my name!* he thought as he sat straight and proud on his horse. But he nodded with humility and gratitude.

Andromache and Astyanax were waiting for him in the palace courtyard. The day ended in much the same way as it had begun, except now Hector had a victory and the knowledge that he'd been correct all along. *Now,* he knew, *we'll win this war.*

Later that night, in the Greek camp...

THE EMISSARY

NESTOR SIGHED DEEPLY as he walked with Odysseus and Diomedes. *If we lose this war because two commanders can't get along,* he thought, *then may the bards sing of Greek obstinance for all eternity.*

After the tragedy that was the fall of the trench, Agamemnon presented a lengthy tirade to the commanders. Nestor sat and listened while he spoke about how the Trojans took just one morning to destroy a trench that had taken the Greeks years to dig. For hours he wouldn't let anyone else talk until, finally, he grew tired.

Nestor, mostly because of his advanced age, felt safe enough to be the first to speak. His message was clear: They didn't lose the trench because they were inferior soldiers and ill prepared. They lost the trench because they weren't working together. Nestor emphasized that they needed Achilles and the Myrmidons. This prompted another prolonged argument over the merits of Achilles.

In the end, Agamemnon was defeated by Nestor's arguments and his own lack of energy. Since the men had seen their side lose honor so spectacularly, Agamemnon conceded to allow an emissary to apologize to Achilles on his behalf.

Nestor, Odysseus, and Diomedes were chosen the most likely to get through to Achilles. Nestor could tell by their faces that none of them were excited about the task. They took a small entourage bearing gifts from Agamemnon and headed toward the Myrmidon camp.

They found Achilles and Patroclus eating. Achilles didn't look excited to see them, but Patroclus, being his normal hospitable self, asked them to sit and drink wine.

"How bad is it?" Achilles asked. "Patroclus has heard some rumors, but we didn't really want to know the reality until we had a night of sleep."

"Sorry to interrupt your sleep," Nestor said. "But it's bad. We lost the trench. The Trojans were joined by the Dardanians. They pushed us back behind our wall."

"How many Greeks dead?" Patroclus asked. "Are there any wounded?"

"We aren't sure exactly," Odysseus replied. "We're gathering the bodies and will have a funeral pyre later tonight. It will be more than five thousand, though. Hector killed probably a quarter of them. He's fierce."

"The wounded are back in the camp," Diomedes said. "They're being looked after by your healers, Patroclus. We'll need more healers tomorrow, I think. The Trojans are sure to hit us again while we're down. They'll come at the wall with full force in the morning."

"That's why we're here," Nestor said. "Achilles, Agamemnon sends his sincere apology. Outside, there are servants with food, wine, and gold—gifts from Agamemnon."

Achilles didn't say anything. He just raised his eyebrows and took a drink of wine. Nestor looked at Patroclus, but he couldn't read his face at all. *Oh, I hope this works,* Nestor thought. *For all our sakes.*

"One more thing," Odysseus said as he clapped his hands. "Agamemnon sends this token of his apology."

A servant entered the tent, escorting a clean and healthy-looking Briseis. Both Achilles and Patroclus stood immediately and ran to her. They embraced one another.

How strange. Both of them love her, Nestor reflected. *She must be quite a woman.*

"Are you hurt?" Patroclus asked Briseis.

"No," she answered. "I never even saw Agamemnon. I stayed in the women's tent all night. He called for others, but not for me."

"Patroclus," Achilles said, "take Briseis and get something to eat outside this tent."

Patroclus began, "Achilles, I really think that—"

Achilles interrupted in a soft voice. "Patroclus, take Briseis so that I can talk to these men."

They left.

Achilles sat down with Nestor, Odysseus, and Diomedes. "Thank you for coming," he said. "Thank you for bringing her safely back. But, my answer is still no. I made a vow, and I'll uphold that vow. The Myrmidons will not fight for Greece."

"Please listen," Nestor began. "I appeal to you. You don't know what it was like today. Hector is relentless— there was no way to stop him. Our army is demoralized by Agamemnon. And then there's Aeneas. He's the son of Aphrodite. We can't fight him without our own son of an Immortal. You must bring the Myrmidons to refresh our army's energy. We beg of you."

"Achilles," Odysseus added, "these are your people who are dying. Your father's countrymen are among the dead. You can help us stop the death. You must fight tomorrow. You must have honor."

"Honor?" Achilles said. "All of this is about honor. My honor. Why does Agamemnon get to decide when to keep and give up his honor while I don't? I took an oath in front of all of you, in front of all of Greece, that I will not lead the Myrmidons in further battle against the Trojans. My honor demands that I respect my own words."

"Agamemnon is foolish and worried that his men will think him weak," said Diomedes. "Your men will never see you as weak, even if you break your oath and join us to fight. You know that. Your men revere you."

"It's not my men I'm thinking of," Achilles replied. "It's myself. He used my name to lure Iphigenia to her death. He disregarded my advice about the length of the war. He took Briseis because of his selfish need to save face. He did all of these dishonorable things and gets away with it! At some point, someone must refuse him. I must refuse him. Leave me now. I'm getting physically sick that the three of you still serve him."

I must try to appeal, Nestor thought. "Is there no way, Achilles?" he asked. "Can you let your father's people die? Can you truly disregard the fact that you're as a part of Greece as the soil of Delphi? If you look into my eyes and tell me that there is no way, then we'll leave in peace."

Achilles got up from his chair and took another seat right next to Nestor. He pulled Nestor's chair toward him, then grabbed Nestor's face and brought it close to his own. Nestor looked deep in Achilles's eyes.

"Nestor," Achilles said, "most wise Nestor, friend to all of Greece, I tell you that there is absolutely no way that I'll lead the Myrmidons to help the Greeks."

He won't budge. I can see it, Nestor thought.

Dejected, the three men walked sluggishly back across the camp.

One week later...

THE FATE OF PATROCLUS

S EVERAL DAYS PASSED. Each day brought Patroclus news of more Greek defeats and deaths. The wounded were so plentiful now that Briseis and he hardly slept. He hadn't openly discussed the situation with Achilles, even though he was tempted on several occasions. Patroclus knew that something had to change, or the Myrmidons would have to sail alone and leave the dead behind. *I'm worried that we'll have to return to Greece and leave the rest of the army behind,* he thought. *How will we face our people?*

Briseis told Patroclus that he was looking too tired and ragged to be considered healthy. She ordered him to have an entire evening away from healing. He had a nice dinner with Achilles and slept well for the first time since the trench fell.

When he woke, he could tell from the light that it was at least midmorning. *I've slept late,* he thought. *Briseis was correct. I needed a night of rest.*

Achilles was still asleep beside him. With no fighting to do, Achilles had taken to sleeping well into the morning. Patroclus crawled out of Achilles's strong arms, put on a tunic, and walked outside to get air. He saw three streams of black smoke rising over the Aegean.

The Myrmidon camp was itself still largely asleep. Patroclus didn't see much activity when he looked around for someone to ask about the smoke. Then a Greek soldier in full armor rode on a horse near the camp. Patroclus walked in his direction and waved for the horseman to stop.

"Where is that smoke coming from?" Patroclus asked him.

"The Trojans broke through our wall this morning," he answered. "They cleared a path through our camp and made it all the way to the beach. They've set some of our ships on fire."

"They cleared a path? That means they've killed their way through."

"Yes, sir. Lots of Greeks have fallen. But I must go. I have communication for Odysseus."

The soldier raced away on his horse. Patroclus noticed that a fourth stream of smoke was now reaching toward the sky. He went back inside the tent and found Achilles sitting on the edge of the bed.

"I heard," Achilles said.

"What can we do?"

"There's nothing to do. When the fighting stops, you and Briseis can go to help."

"Achilles," Patroclus said softly, "I've stayed out of this stalemate with Agamemnon. But I can't any longer. Too many are hurt and dead."

"What are you asking me?"

"Achilles, you must lead the Myrmidons into battle. Just the sight of you coming into action will rally the Greeks. I think the Trojans have set fire to only four ships so far. But what happens if they burn the whole fleet?"

"Patroclus," Achilles said, "you know that I'm not an evil person."

"Of course I do. I know that you don't do this lightly and that every drop of Greek blood hurts you to your core. I know that you must have something, deep inside, that's keeping you to your vow. Is it just about your honor? I don't think so. There must be more."

Achilles sighed deeply and said, "It's my mother. She's an Immortal—she can see and hear when and where she wants. I can give up my honor and disavow my word. I can do this for you and the other soldiers. But I can't let her see me purposefully give up honor. I would feel like I was turning my back on everything she ever taught me. The rest of you have the privilege of doing things that would disappoint your mothers because they'll never, ever know. I don't have that privilege. It's the burden of being born to an Immortal."

I never thought about it like that, Patroclus thought. *She knows all he says and does. I could dishonor my father by stealing a thousand horses and lying about it directly to his face. But Achilles can never do that to his mother, it's impossible. I finally realize that Thetis would never understand why he would choose to support the Greeks when Agamemnon doesn't deserve it. He can't go back on his word. However, perhaps there's another way.*

"Then, Achilles," Patroclus said, "let me do it. I'll put on your armor and lead the Myrmidons. The only people who will know it's me will be you and your mother, who sees all. It's the perfect solution. The apparent sight of you will rally the Myrmidons and the Greeks. All the while, your mother will know that you're sticking to your word that you won't lead the Myrmidons into battle against Troy."

"With all due respect, Patroclus," Achilles said, "the Myrmidons, the Greeks, and the Trojans will surely realize that it's not me in the armor."

"With all due respect, Achilles," Patroclus said, "I've spent a lifetime watching your every move. When I was young, I did nothing except study your body and every muscle in it. Don't forget that I was also trained by Chiron. I can do this."

"It's dangerous and I can't allow it."

"I'm not going to do any real fighting. I know how to use the sword as you do, to give energy to the men. I'll stay away from any danger."

Achilles sat in silence. *This must be how Odysseus feels,* Patroclus thought, *to have the perfect solution—the most clever way of accomplishing two opposing actions at the same time.*

Finally, Achilles said, "All right. But you'll be in a chariot—I'm not compromising on that. If you're driving a chariot, it will give you reason to keep a small distance from Trojan foot soldiers."

Patroclus nodded. Achilles got up and started to dress him in the armor. Patroclus felt great empowerment as the heavy armor pressed against him. *This armor has experienced a part of Achilles that I never have. Now, I'll get that honor,* he thought. Achilles gave Patroclus instructions on how to use the sword, but Patroclus didn't need, or pay attention to, this lecture.

Achilles sent for his chariot.

"You have no need to be a hero," Achilles said. "Do not engage in the fight, no matter how tempting it may be. Stay away from the walls of Troy, as their archers are too accurate. If the battle gets out of control, find Odysseus and show him who you are. He'll protect you. Do you understand?"

"Yes," Patroclus answered.

Patroclus started moving toward the opening of the tent. Suddenly, Achilles grabbed him from behind and held him close. He put his hands on the helmet to make sure that Patroclus was well protected. Patroclus had never felt more proud of himself in his life. When Achilles released him, he walked through the opening and jumped onto the waiting chariot. He grabbed the reins and started moving.

It took only a moment for a few Myrmidons to notice him. They started shouting loudly. Soon, the entire Myrmidon camp was awake and moving quickly. Patroclus ran the chariot back and forth in front of the camp. The Myrmidons didn't need instruction as they buckled and tied themselves into armor. Patroclus knew the commanders, and he motioned to them the same way that Achilles would have. The entire camp exploded with action. *They've been waiting for this moment*, he told himself.

The Myrmidons, some on horseback and some on foot, moved swiftly as a group. They gained speed and raced toward the Greek camp. Patroclus soon saw the surprised looks of the Greek soldiers, followed by their cheers of encouragement. *It's happening. I feel the energy. The power of Achilles is fueling a great charge.*

They neared the place where the Trojans had created a path through the camp. A large Trojan soldier was orchestrating the movement of the others. Patroclus knew it was time to turn back and let the Myrmidons proceed, but before he could, the large soldier grabbed the horse that pulled Patroclus's chariot. The chariot came to a stop. The man took a spear and held it firmly with the point pressed against Patroclus.

"Mighty Achilles," the man said in a deep voice. "I want you to know who I am. Everyone must remember the name of the man who has finally killed you. I am Sarpedon of Lycia, son of Zeus."

Don't waste time, Patroclus told himself. *Do what Achilles would do—always be fast with no room for indecision. Use everything you have at your disposal.*

Patroclus leaned forward and hit his horse with the flat part of his blade. The horse jerked forward, causing Sarpedon to lose his grip. As the chariot moved past, Patroclus swiped his sword and cut Sarpedon in the leg. It wasn't a deep cut, but it caused enough pain that Sarpedon dropped his spear and fell to the ground.

Don't waste time, Patroclus thought. He stopped his horse, jumped from the chariot, and stabbed Sarpedon in the back of the neck. Blood spurted out and Sarpedon fell completely into the dirt. *That's it for him,* Patroclus realized. *I've seen enough wounds to know that he's as good as dead. No healer can fix this wound—I should know.*

He jumped back on the chariot and quickly took off. The Myrmidons loudly shouted their congratulations around him. The Greeks became even more energized. Patroclus turned the chariot and rode directly for the Greek wall, splitting the Trojans on either side of the path. When he exited the Greek camp, he noticed that the Trojans were not prepared to defend their side of the wall. Patroclus steered next to the wall, stopped his horse, and took a break.

He watched as the Greeks pushed the Trojans out and back across the trench. Patroclus looked for Hector but didn't see him. *Where's Hector?* he wondered. *I've killed Sarpedon, son of Zeus himself! I'm a hero.*

Patroclus knew it was wrong and against the wishes of Achilles, but he wanted more. The Trojans were scattering in all directions. They began to close the gate to the city. Patroclus started forward on the chariot and continued, at full speed, toward the walls of Troy. He passed Trojan soldiers, who stared at him and seemed in awe of his boldness.

Despite the fact that he was surrounded by Trojans, Patroclus reached the wall. He felt strong and proud as Achilles's armor pressed against him. *I'll climb over their precious wall and open the gate.* Arrows began to fly past him. He jumped from the chariot and ran so that he was too close to the wall for the archers to get a good aim. He'd trained with Achilles for so long that it was not hard for him to get a footing on one of the stone blocks. He climbed, pausing briefly to look behind him.

The Greeks, led by Menelaus, were almost to him. *They're ready to attack when I open the gate,* he thought. Patroclus climbed up three more blocks, then he felt an enormous weight pulling on his body. He looked down, but nothing was there. *Am I getting tired?* The weight became too great, and he fell to the ground. He stood quickly but was immediately knocked down, this time by a person. He opened his eyes and saw Hector standing over him.

"It's a great honor to kill Achilles," Hector said. "I've waited for this moment for a long while."

Hector took his sword and stabbed Patroclus through an opening in the side of the armor. Immediately, Patroclus tasted blood. *This is the end. I know enough to know that. Achilles, forgive me.*

Hector dropped down. "Your armor is mine," he said. "I'll give it someday to my son." He grabbed the helmet and removed it. Then his face went blank.

"I'm not Achilles," Patroclus said. "You haven't killed a great hero. Just a normal person."

"I know who you are," Hector said. "And you aren't a normal person. You're Patroclus, the love of Achilles."

"And he'll punish you and all of Troy for this."

"You're right," Hector said dejectedly. "I'm so sorry. I haven't killed Achilles, but I've probably sealed the fate of many of my own men, including myself. Achilles will make us pay for what I've accidentally done to you, Patroclus. I've probably just as good as destroyed Troy itself."

Achilles, forgive me for being arrogant, Patroclus thought. *I went against my nature, and it has cost me my life.* He felt Hector slowly stripping the armor from him. *Thetis, Immortal of the sea, thank you for Achilles. At least I'll never know a world without him. I'm most grateful for that.*

Shortly after, back in the Myrmidon camp…

THE DESPAIR OF ACHILLES

ACHILLES WENT OUTSIDE when he heard his name being called. It was Nestor's son, Antilochus. He knew from the way that the voice sounded that something bad had occurred. *He was sent to deliver a message to me,* Achilles thought. *Only one message meant for me would make his voice sound like that.* He knew exactly what it was, but he could not admit it to himself. *I need to hear the words said, or it isn't real. Can I make it not be real?*

"Achilles," Antilochus said in an extremely shaky voice, "did you know that Patroclus was wearing your armor?"

I know what it is. I know. "Yes, of course," Achilles said.

"Hector thought that he was you. Hector killed him."

"Patroclus is dead?"

"Yes."

Of course he is. Patroclus is dead because Hector thought that he was me. How do I live in a world where this has happened?

Antilochus walked up to him and tried to catch him as he fell. But Achilles, in the process of throwing himself on the ground, pushed Antilochus away.

"Leave me!" Achilles yelled. He rolled over until he was face down in the sand and dirt. It was hard to breathe, but he didn't care. *I don't ever want to see the sun again.* He screamed loudly into the ground. He never thought about others looking at him. He pounded the dirt with his fists and kicked his bare feet, as if he were a child denied a trinket. The dirt flew into his open mouth as he continued to scream into the ground.

Then he smelled salt water and knew his mother was close. He felt her hands on the back of his head. She crouched down next to him.

"Achilles," Thetis said softly, "I've come to help you."

"I don't need any help!" he yelled into the sand. "Nothing has changed."

"Patroclus has died. Everything has changed."

"No, it's a mistake. He'll be coming back any moment now, wearing my armor."

"Achilles, Patroclus is dead. You must believe it."

Achilles lifted his head from the ground and stared at his mother with wide eyes. She still held his head in a firm embrace.

"How dare you say this to me!" Achilles yelled. "I must not believe it! Other people can believe such things when they hear of death. But do not align Patroclus with other people. He's extraordinary. Let others believe such things, but not me."

"Yes," Thetis said. "He was extraordinary. And, now, so is your grief. I can feel it, Achilles. There's a fire burning inside you—a real fire that grows with every moment. I don't like this. The fire is unlike anything I've seen before."

"Then bring him back! You're an Immortal. Make it happen."

"No Immortal, not even Zeus, can do such a thing. Patroclus is dead."

Achilles turned his head against the ground again and yelled, "Stop saying Patroclus is dead!" *I said it. Patroclus is dead,* he thought. *I said those words, and now I can't deny it.*

Achilles began to sob loudly. Thetis grabbed his head and supported it. He started to cough from the dirt he'd inhaled. She held him, like a baby, as he sobbed and coughed.

"Breathe," Thetis said, "breathe deep and even."

"Breathe?" Achilles said as he stood quickly. "How can I breathe when he can't? Nothing you have to say makes it better. Perhaps you should just go."

"I'll go," Thetis said. "I don't have the ability to help you, I see that now. But I'll keep watch over you until help does come along. However, Achilles, before I go, there's something that you must do."

"Leave!" Achilles shouted. "I'll do nothing! I wish I could die right now."

"Listen to me, Achilles. This is important. You must listen. Hector has taken your armor and retreated into Troy. The Trojans and Greeks are now fighting a fierce battle for the body of Patroclus. The Greeks want it so that they can give him a proper funeral. The Trojans want to defile the body of the man who was so close to the mighty Achilles, who killed so many. Achilles, you must go to the place where Patroclus lies. He must have a funeral pyre, or he won't be able to cross the River Styx."

He still has a body. No one should touch it except me, Achilles thought. *She's right. I must have his body. I must!*

"How can I do this?" Achilles said urgently. "My armor is gone. All I wear is a simple loincloth. How can I successfully fight to get Patroclus back when I have no weapon?"

"You won't need armor or weapons. Go to the place where the body is, and Athena will help you. She has promised me. The Trojans just need to see you, and they'll flee. Go!"

Achilles watched his mother as she walked across the beach and entered the sea. There were other men around who had seen the entire display. They stood in wonder and stared at him.

He started walking at a steady pace. He wasn't thinking anything, he was only feeling. He just kept walking through the Greek camp. He was barefoot and carried no weapons. He remained dressed in only the loincloth. He didn't pay any attention to how the other soldiers reacted to him.

Achilles stepped through an opening in the Greek wall. On the other side of the trench, he saw Menelaus thrashing Trojans with his sword. Menelaus stood over Patroclus's body. He was doing everything possible to keep the Trojans away. Simultaneously, Achilles felt hatred for the Trojans and gratitude for Menelaus.

He walked down into the trench and easily stepped up the other side. The sun was setting and the sky was absolutely stunning, with reds and oranges on full display. As he appeared from the trench, he looked down and saw that his skin was dancing with burning flames. *I don't feel hot and there's no burning, but my skin is alive with fire. This must be Athena.*

When he finally cleared the trench, he looked at a dead soldier and caught a glimpse of his reflection in the soldier's shiny shield. Achilles's entire body had flames shooting from it, and his head looked as though he wore a crown of flames.

"Patroclus!" Achilles shouted.

The very air shook with the passion of Achilles, Patroclus, and Athena. The Trojans reacted immediately with terrified screams as they ran toward their city. Menelaus was stunned. Suddenly, all was silent. Not even nature made a sound. The Aegean was as still as a pond, and every bird lost its song.

Achilles picked up Patroclus and walked steadily back to their tent. He bathed Patroclus, rubbed him with scented oils, and laid him on the bed. Achilles lay next to him. He lost all track of time as he forced himself to stay awake. He focused his eyes on Patroclus's skin, pale and dry. At some point, Achilles heard Briseis enter the tent.

"Please leave us alone," Achilles said. "I don't even want you to look at us."

"I've brought you some food," Briseis said through tears. "Oh, Patroclus, I love you."

Achilles opened his eyes briefly and saw that Briseis had fallen to the ground. She was crying. *I can't take all this crying*, he thought. "Briseis," he said in a calm voice, "you must leave us. Take the food with you. I'll never eat again. I'll never drink again. I will not bathe and I will not sleep. These things are for the living, of which I am not."

The next morning…

THE WRATH OF
ACHILLES BEGINS

A s WAS HIS promise, Achilles had not slept all night. He lay next to Patroclus and lamented the
coldness of his skin. He saw Briseis enter the tent
to check on them, but he quickly dismissed her each time.
She left food and wine for him that he did not touch.

Then he saw the beginnings of sunlight. *The first sunrise that Patroclus won't see,* he thought. He noticed a movement through the tent opening that was not Briseis. He
smelled the salt water.

"Mother," Achilles said, "what are you doing here?
You'll certainly have no words of wisdom that I need. It's
insulting that an Immortal wants to tell me about grief."

"I didn't come to talk," Thetis said. "I came to help
you on the path that you've set yourself on. Last night, I,
against all sense, went to Mount Olympus. Zeus has for-
bidden the Immortals from offering assistance to you in
retribution for Patroclus killing Sarpedon. But Athena helped me in my quest to seek Hephaestus. I asked Hephaestus, the only Immortal who can wield fire and metal, to
make new armor for you. He went to work straight away.

I've never seen one work so furiously. I asked him why he worked so hard for you. He told me that there were two reasons. First, there's a fire inside you, Achilles, that he can't resist. He's compelled and drawn to you. Second, he had a great respect for Patroclus and wanted to honor him by protecting you."

Thetis moved aside and revealed the armor that had been placed on the table. Achilles got up and studied it. He lifted the helmet.

"It's heavy," he said. "What is it?"

"It's made from iron. There's none other like it in the world."

Achilles felt the heavy iron that had been overlaid with bronze and gold. The design was stunning and mimicked human anatomy. He knew that the armor would exactly fit his muscles.

"And here's the shield," Thetis said.

Achilles went to it. Even in his current irrational state, he stood in awe. The top of the shield depicted the night sky. Each star was exactly in the correct place. Under the sky, Hephaestus had sculpted the entirety of human existence. There were hunters, lovers, farmers, seafarers, children, elderly—all of them meticulously made. Achilles noticed two complete villages on the shield. One was at war and one was at peace. The shield contained all of the human experience.

"The shield is a masterpiece," Thetis said. "Even among the Immortals there's nothing like it. Now go. I know that the fire calls to you from within."

She helped Achilles put on the armor. When they went outside, he watched her walk to the sea. He didn't call for the Myrmidons to rise up. *Whoever wants to fight, may,* he thought. *I don't care. All the Greeks can sleep and let me kill more Trojans than they would have combined.*

Then he shouted, loudly, to anyone who might hear, "No one is to enter my tent! No one is to even think about touching Patroclus. My mother will tell me if anyone violates this decree. Whoever touches Patroclus will find that he, and his entire company, will be dead within an hour."

He took the first chariot that he came to and rode as fast as he could through the Greek wall, over the trench, and toward Troy.

He couldn't realize time in his state. He could only realize whatever person he was killing in that moment. Then he continued on to the next.

The River Scamander flowed near Troy and had been a source of water for the Greeks. Achilles found that he was most efficient if he stood at the river and let the Trojans come to him. After he killed a soldier, he pushed the body quickly over the edge of the bank. In this way, he could kill the next without the burden of bodies piling up around him.

He smiled when he noticed that the river held more blood than water. The bodies acted like a dam and caused the river to flood upstream. *The river looks angry. Good,* he thought. *I'll fight even the river if I have to.*

Eventually, the sun sank in the sky and he walked back to the Greek camp. He killed as he walked. *I haven't met Hector yet. Where is he?*

He came upon a young soldier, no more than fifteen years old, wearing the royal armor of a prince of Troy. Achilles kicked the prince and then pinned him to the ground with his foot. He retrieved his sword and was about to strike.

"Where's Hector?" Achilles asked.

"I don't know," the prince said, afraid. "Somewhere by the Greek trench, probably."

Achilles lifted his blade.

"Stop," the prince begged. "Please don't. I'm a son of Priam. I'm young, but there are few of us left, and he needs all the sons he has. Don't kill me. Take me as a prisoner and ransom me to my father. He will pay handsomely for me."

Achilles took a moment to ponder, then said, "Young prince, there was a time when I would have done just that. But that time has passed. As I look down at you, I see that Patroclus was so much better than you—in every way. If I'm not to get any money for Patroclus, who was clearly better, then why should I want money for you?"

Achilles drove his blade into the boy's throat. He proceeded to sit down next the prince and listened to his throat gurgle until he finally died. Achilles called the nearest Greek soldier and gave him the gift of the prince's armor.

He got off the ground and continued walking back to his tent. Now that his mind wasn't occupied with killing, he was able to notice those around him. He saw that the soldiers stared at his armor in wonder. He took off his helmet and allowed his golden hair to accent the sculpted shoulders that he wore. Nobody approached him, not even the Myrmidon commanders he was closest to.

Briseis was in the tent when he arrived. Patroclus hadn't been touched, and Achilles nodded with implied gratitude toward her. She began to help him take off his armor, but he pushed her away. He removed the armor and placed it on a table.

"I'll get water," Briseis said. "You're covered in blood and must wash."

"No!" Achilles shouted. "I will not bathe. You may clean the armor, out of respect for Hephaestus, but I will not bathe—I made a vow not to."

"Achilles," Briseis said, "you must at least wash off all the blood that comes from so many different soldiers. You'll ruin your bed."

"I don't care. And Patroclus, obviously, won't care. So if no one in this bed will care, then why does it matter?"

"You're wrong," Briseis said boldly. "Patroclus would care. Patroclus wouldn't want this for you. He'd want you to be clean and to eat."

"How dare you?" Achilles said. "You'll tell me about what Patroclus wants? No. Only I know what he wants."

"I loved him too," Briseis pleaded.

"You're just like my mother!" Achilles shouted. "You try to make him seem ordinary—as if he were just another person people loved. You didn't love him as I did! He wasn't ordinary. Now go!"

Briseis left and Achilles crawled into the bed next to Patroclus.

One week later…

PATROCLUS COMES
TO ACHILLES

S EVEN DAYS HAD passed since the death of Patroclus, and there had not been any change in Achilles. He continued his abstinence from food, drink, sleep, and hygiene. And despite his obstinance, he continued his daily reign of terror on the Trojans.

He saw Hector several times from a distance, but he was never able to get close enough to him in time. Hector commanded the Trojan forces to retake the Greek trench. *They must be desperate*, Achilles thought. *Or Hector would never continue this bloodbath*. It was in the trench that Achilles killed hundreds upon hundreds each day.

Achilles learned that Odysseus had successfully placed a spy within the royal court of Priam. This spy informed the Greeks that Priam wanted to call off the Trojan offensive, retreat, and close the gates. But Hector was defiant and insistent on proving that an offensive would work. Thus, Achilles was given the golden opportunity to destroy the enemy one man at a time, as quickly as he could.

At night, Achilles lay next to Patroclus on the bed with his eyes open. One night, surprisingly, Achilles found that he was having a dream. *How can one have a dream while still awake?* he wondered. *Is it possible?* But no matter how hard he tried, he could not stop the dream from coming into his consciousness. He could see both the events of the dream and the real tent around him at the same time.

He dreamed that he was sitting on a boulder outside the cave of Chiron. The horse sculpture was next to him. He was watching Patroclus stack logs on a pile. Achilles admired Patroclus's body. Then Patroclus stopped his task and came over to where Achilles was sitting.

"Achilles," the dream Patroclus said, "you must burn my body on a funeral pyre. I can't cross over the river until you do this, and I'm tired. Your mother is tired, too."

"What does my mother have to do with it?" Achilles asked.

"Haven't you noticed that my body doesn't decay? And haven't you wondered how you're able to have such strength without eating for so many days? Your mother comes into the tent at night. She makes you sleep. Then she introduces nectar and ambrosia, the food of the Immortals, directly into our bodies. The food keeps me from decay and you from weakness. But she grows tired of making the journey to Mount Olympus to get the nectar and ambrosia. Please, Achilles, give my body the proper funeral rite."

Why do the people I love keep stopping me from staying true to my word? Achilles wondered. *I didn't want to eat, drink, or sleep, yet she forces it upon me. But how can I maintain anger at Mother when part of her goal is just to keep Patroclus pristine for his funeral? Nothing about making an oath is ever easy.*

Then, as fast as it had begun, the dream was over and Achilles was completely in the tent. Chiron's cave was gone. He tried desperately to go back to the dream, to go back to the horse sculpture. He remembered the good times there with Patroclus and wanted to relive them.

It's no use, he realized. *The dream is gone forever.* He rose and walked outside. He saw Briseis sleeping on the ground by the fire. He shook her a bit to wake her.

"Briseis," Achilles said, "I won't fight today. I'll stay with Patroclus all day. Please don't disturb me. However, I have some tasks for you. Instruct the Myrmidon commanders to construct a large funeral pyre. Try to find a raised location on the plain where a man can see the Aegean. Build the structure there. We'll have the funeral rites when the sun goes down. Find a priest of Athena, but make sure he has never set foot inside the tent of Agamemnon. You may be present at the pyre. Besides yourself, only Nestor, Antilochus, and Menelaus are allowed."

Achilles noticed a sigh of relief come from Briseis. He saw in her eyes a look of gratitude and love. She didn't say anything, and he went back into the tent. Achilles spent the entire day in bed, with his arms around Patroclus.

The dream is gone.

When the time was right, Achilles carried Patroclus outside and followed Briseis to the place she had chosen. *It's perfect*, he thought. *She did well. I can hear the sounds of the sea.* In the moonlight, he saw his mother walk out of the water. Thetis did not come all the way to the pyre. She just stood there on the beach. Achilles climbed the pyre and placed Patroclus on top.

The priest said the ritual words. Achilles felt the fire within him begin to dwindle. *How strange*, he reflected. *Just at the time that the pyre is lit, my own fire dies.*

The priest motioned for Achilles to place the torch on the structure. But he couldn't do it.

"You protected his body," Achilles said to Menelaus. "I saw you that day as you took great pain to make sure no Trojan got close. I don't know why you did it, but you surely are the better brother. Please do Patroclus the honor of lighting the pyre."

Menelaus bowed deeply. Achilles saw a glistening in his eyes. Then the pyre was lit. The flames grew fast and engulfed the wood. *I can't see Patroclus anymore,* Achilles thought.

They all stood there and watched. Briseis could not take the emotion. She fell to the ground and wailed. None of them attempted to comfort her.

"We'll call for a respite from battle," Nestor said. "Out of respect for Patroclus, we'll hold funeral games."

Going back to normal? Achilles wondered. *How can that be?*

"No!" he yelled as the others jumped out of fear. "Did you think that this funeral would change something? It has not! You all thought that I would go back to being regular Achilles. Well, you're sorely mistaken. I'm resolved as ever to kill every last Trojan. Tomorrow I'll begin with Hector."

"No, Achilles," Nestor said. "This must stop. We've all been watching you, but none of us have had the courage to talk to you. Well, my age is in my favor. What is it to me if you kill me and throw me on the pyre with Patroclus?"

"Say what you want, old man," Achilles said. "It won't make a difference to me."

"Here's what's being said in the Greek camp. We wonder why you rage when others have had it so much worse. There are those who have lost entire families! Some have lost parts of their own body. You've lost one person, and you rage as if you've lost your kingdom. Also, death isn't a cause for such a reaction. The Immortals themselves call for death and know our fate. Patroclus is in a much better state. He doesn't have to feel hot or suffer the pain of the cold anymore. He'll never have another toothache or feel a festering wound. He's better off where he is."

Achilles listened to Nestor. But each word added dry timber to his soul. The fire within him now raged higher than the pyre of Patroclus.

"Don't you ever talk to me like that again!" Achilles shouted with such force that the ground shook. "So, I don't have it as bad as others? None of you knew Patroclus! Again, why do you Greeks keep making Patroclus an ordinary person? He wasn't. Not even the man who watched his own children be slaughtered in front of him knows my pain. Not even the man who lost a kingdom. Then, you tell me that the Immortals demand death—as if that's supposed to help somehow. I know the Immortals better than any of you. I talk to one often! They know nothing of death. But, on top of all of this, you tell me that Patroclus is better off not having a toothache than being with me. Go away. All of you."

Achilles stood, rigid, and stared at the fire. He didn't know how long the others stayed. Sometime during the middle of the night, he left the smoldering wood and walked back to his tent. He stayed extra alert on this night, just in case his mother dared to come with nectar and ambrosia.

That same night...

ODYSSEUS PLOTS

ODYSSEUS SAW PATROCLUS'S funeral pyre from a distance. *Goodbye, healer,* he thought. *You really were the best of us all.* He was wearing all black and continued on a path toward the walls of Troy. He stayed to the shadows and silently checked his surroundings to make certain he was alone.

As he crossed the plain, the smell of death was everywhere. The Trojans hadn't been able to keep up with the pace of Achilles's killing. Bodies had been left to decompose on the ground. *At least we've always been able to send our dead on their way across the river,* he thought.

He reached his destination, the first grove of trees on the edge of the plain. He walked into the trees and saw a dark figure standing among them.

"The owl hoots loud tonight," Odysseus said.

"It's loud enough to kill a horse," the figure replied.

That's right, Odysseus thought. Then he asked, "Any news?"

"Once in a great while," the man began, "a spy comes across information so valuable that he can't wait to share it."

"Is your impatience due to your desire to help Greece? Or is your impatience due to the hope that the information warrants a high payment?"

"Both, my king," the spy said.

At least he's honest, Odysseus thought. *I appreciate that.* "Which is greater?" he asked. "Your love of Greece or your desire for money?"

"It doesn't really matter when I'm sure to have both. Yes, I have news that's valuable enough for me to be boastful. It will help assure a Greek victory. And, of course, I won't turn down the extra gold."

"Tell me," said Odysseus. "If it's as good as you claim, I'll leave golden dishes with your brother."

"I've worked for years to gain the trust of the priest of Apollo. Priam relies on this man constantly, and I always wanted to know the things that they speak of. It's taken quite a while. But, ten nights ago, there was a breakthrough. The priest was tired, and I offered to take him to my quarters to make dinner. He accepted. We ate and drank—I made sure it was the strongest wine in all of Troy. I got him to talk."

"Can he be trusted?" Odysseus asked. "Perhaps he was fooling you."

"He would have no reason to make up the things he told me. If they weren't true, there would be no benefit for Troy and no disadvantage for us. They must be true. He told me that Apollo himself created two conditions that must be met before Troy can fall. If both of these happen, Troy can be destroyed."

"What are they?" Odysseus asked.

"First, the arrows of Heracles must come to Troy and be used to kill the heir. Do these arrows still exist?"

"I'm not sure. But I can certainly find out—I have an idea where they could be. It's said that they're poisoned arrows dipped into the blood of the Hydra."

"Yes," the spy said. "You must get them and use them to kill Hector."

Or the next heir, if Achilles has his way, Odysseus thought. Then he asked, "What's the second prophecy?"

"This one is harder. The son of Achilles must be brought to the fight. He must kill the king of Troy."

"Really?" Odysseus said. "Now, that's certainly more interesting than the arrows. You're right, the priest would have no reason to make these things up."

"It's impossible, isn't it? There's no way that Achilles can have a son. Everyone knows that—"

"There are secrets, my friend. And sometimes, those secrets have secrets."

"Then what about my gold?"

"You shall get it," Odysseus said. "You have done well. Now, there's a rumor you need to plant. I've been working on a plan. I won't explain it, but all you need to do is spread a rumor at the court of Priam. Give it to the servants and see that it works its way up. The rumor is that Odysseus is having a feud with several Lyrnessian slaves. The slaves have staged a revolt over a construction project that Odysseus is working on. There's instability in the Greek camp. Make sure that all the princes and Priam himself hear that there's a revolt over a construction project."

"Is that it?" the spy asked. "Why tell the enemy that your own men fight amongst themselves?"

"Rumors are seeds. Even the oak tree has an insignificant beginning that most people ignore."

The next morning...

THE FATE OF HECTOR

T HE SUN CAME through the palace window and woke Hector. For the first time in over a moon, he'd slept well. Andromache and Astyanax breathed peacefully beside him. The night before, Hector had noticed a funeral pyre on the plain near the sea. Priam's spies went to work, and he eventually found out that the funeral was for Patroclus. *He's finally come to his senses,* Hector thought. *The body must have been in a terrible condition.*

Hector assumed that the Greeks would take some time to formally mourn and hold games in Patroclus's honor. Then, a knock on the bedroom door gave him the suspicion that his assumption was incorrect.

"Come in," Hector said.

One of his commanders, in full armor, entered and said, "I apologize for waking you, Prince Hector. Achilles is on a chariot right in front of the gate. He's been calling your name since the sun first came up. The other commanders didn't know what to do, so I woke you."

Andromache sat up in bed, holding the sleeping Astyanax. Hector got out of the bed. He didn't care if the commander saw him naked.

"Is Achilles alone?" Hector asked.

"Yes, mostly. Some of the Greek soldiers have naturally come out to watch. I don't see anything organized, though. It looks like a duel challenge to me. I don't think there will be a full battle today."

Hector told the man to go and called for his servant with his armor. He went to a washbasin and poured water over his head. It was cold.

"What do you intend to do?" Andromache asked.

"You know what I have to do," Hector answered.

"You don't have to do anything," Andromache said. "You've done no direct harm to Achilles—you had no way of knowing that another man wore his armor. The rules of a duel are clear. Since there was no direct personal offense, you don't even need to respond. It was a simple mistake that caused the death of the other man."

"I understand that," Hector answered. "I don't act because I feel called by Achilles. I act because it will save many lives. Achilles has obliterated hundreds, even thousands, of my men—good Trojan men. By killing him I'll put an end to his reign of terror."

"I don't agree," Andromache said. "But I can't ask you to be less than you are."

"It's settled then," Hector replied.

Andromache stayed in bed with the baby as a servant helped Hector dress. He put on his best royal armor.

"Wake the palace," Hector instructed the servant, "and alert the army. Everyone needs to be on guard in case this is all a ruse. I don't doubt that the Greeks would try something like this."

Hector put a sword on his belt and walked through the halls of the palace. On the way, he saw Paris and Helen standing in the doorway of their quarters. They bowed to him and stayed silent as he passed. Hector returned the bow, thinking, *If I leave this kingdom to you, Paris, you'd better not ruin it. At least not until Astyanax is old enough to lay claim.*

He crossed the courtyard and looked back briefly at the doors to the great hall. His father stood in the doorway. Priam bowed to him, but Hector stayed erect and continued his walk through the city. Down and down he went on foot. The great horseman didn't have the heart to ride. *All my energy is for one: Achilles.*

He didn't see any Trojan citizens, but he knew that they must be there, peeking out of windows and doors. Word traveled fast in Troy, especially when Achilles was shouting by the gate. Finally, he entered the lowest ring of the city and heard his name being shouted over the wall. Hector had to admit that it was a terrifying sound. He stood by the gate, nodded to a soldier, and waited for the gate to open completely.

Achilles was on his chariot, which was pulled by two magnificent horses. *If I kill him, I'll take his armor and those horses,* Hector thought. *They're almost as good as the Trojan breed.*

Achilles stepped from the chariot and walked toward him. This was the first time that Hector had seen the much-talked-about armor up close. It was as spectacular as described and deserved all the praise it received. *Stop staring at the shield,* he told himself. *Concentrate on the task.*

They didn't speak. Hector soon realized that neither of them intended to waste time with silly posturing and fruitless exercises meant to distract or tire.

Valiant Hector and mighty Achilles fought for the better half the morning. Each had his turn with the upper hand. Each experienced small defeats. However, in the end,

Hector conceded to himself, *No man can win against this Achilles with this armor.*

Then he felt a throbbing pain pierce his side and a sudden sadness descend down his entire body. Achilles had stabbed him and driven his sword to the hilt. Hector fell to the ground. Achilles bent over him.

"I'm honored," Hector said through gurgles of blood, "to have been killed by you, the best warrior that has ever lived. Let them say that Hector was so great, only the greatest could kill him."

"I'm honored by your words," Achilles replied. "I would have liked to have been able to fight beside you. You have the love of your country in your heart. I respect you."

"Then, honor my death. Give my body peacefully to my family so that I may have a proper burial."

"No," Achilles said without hesitation. "You killed Patroclus. As much as I honor you in life, I'll defile your body in death. Let your last thought be the disappointment of never crossing the river. Your family will watch as you sadly degrade. There can be no other way."

Hector felt a pain in his soul greater than any pain of his body. Then, he felt nothing.

Less than a moment later...

DEFILEMENT

ACHILLES STOOD OVER Hector. *Your family will watch as you sadly degrade,* he thought. *Too rough for the last words he'll ever hear? No.* The fire inside Achilles that had been stoked by Patroclus's funeral pyre, and the words of Nestor, was now as hot as ever.

Achilles stripped the royal armor from Hector. He was glad that none of the Trojans were stupid enough to intervene. It wasn't that he wanted to spare lives, he just didn't want anyone interrupting his task.

He threw the armor onto the floor of his chariot and grabbed a rope. Then he dragged Hector by the arm over to the chariot. He tied Hector's hands above his head and fixed them to the back of the chariot. Hector was lying, face up, in the dirt. *Face down would be more defiling,* Achilles thought. *But I want his family to know that it's him.*

Achilles looked up and saw many Trojans watching from the various walls, towers, and parapets of the city. He knew that Priam, Hecuba, Paris, Helen, and Andromache must be among them. *Let them all see what becomes of the man who killed Patroclus.*

Achilles stepped onto the chariot and started to drive. He drove around the entire walled city of Troy, slowly at first, then gaining speed with each pass. Hector's body was dragged through the dirt with each round. Achilles heard wails coming from the city. The wails grew louder as his chariot got faster.

When the sun went down, he drove back to his tent with Hector still attached. The Greeks came out of their tents to watch. When he arrived, Achilles untied Hector and carried him inside. He threw the body in the corner.

Achilles lay on the bed. He'd continued his resolve to refrain from sleeping, eating, drinking, and bathing. It took great energy, but he managed to stay fully alert all night so that his mother could not intervene with food.

It continued this way for several days. In the sun, Achilles dragged Hector around the city and through the dirt. By moonlight, he lay with his eyes open as Hector lay piled in a corner.

No one in the Greek camp dared to disturb this cycle.

Several days later, at night in the Myrmidon camp...

AN OLD MAN COMES
TO ACHILLES

T wo torches dimly lit Achilles's tent. As had become usual, he was on his bed with his eyes open.
The shadowy lump that was Hector lay in the corner. Achilles could hear the sounds of the Myrmidon camp
eating the evening meal. *I hope Briseis has found some
group to eat with,* he thought. He'd grown accustomed to
his current way of life.

Suddenly, the flaps of his tent parted and a tall cloaked
and hooded figure entered. Achilles immediately jumped
out of bed. *Nobody should ever dare to enter this tent now.
My sword is near.*

The figure came into the light of one of the torches and
dropped its hood. It was an elderly man, but he stood erect
and strong. He calmly walked over to Achilles and got
onto his knees. Then the figure took Achilles's hands and
kissed them.

The old man looked up, into Achilles's eyes, and said,
"Now, I've done a thing that nobody else in the world has
done. I've kissed the hands of the man who killed my son.

And the hands that killed many of my other sons, and many of my countrymen."

"Priam?" Achilles asked. "How did you get in here?"

"No one pays attention to an old man," Priam said.

"What are you doing here? You can't have Hector."

"Wanting Hector's body was only one reason I came. The other reason is that this is the only place in the entire Troad where someone won't attempt to console me for the loss of Hector. I'm so weary from others attempting to help me. Nothing helps."

I can understand that, Achilles thought. He helped Priam to his feet and offered him a place at the table. Achilles took a chair across from him.

"I've been told that Hector is in a better place," Priam said. "The priest of Apollo told me that it was the will of the Immortals and I should be glad about it."

"Someone told you that others have suffered far greater losses, didn't they?" Achilles said. "That you should just get over your anger."

"Yes. That one made me so angry, I smashed the queen's favorite vase."

He, of all people, understands. This is extraordinary. He's my enemy. The fire inside Achilles began to wane.

Priam continued. "They also told me to be happy that I have Paris as a replacement heir. As if Paris, as much as I love him, could ever be fit to carry even Hector's dirty tunic."

They sat in silence for several minutes. Achilles considered Priam's face and the honesty he read in it.

"It hurts," Achilles said, finally.

"Yes. You must have loved Patroclus very much. He must have been a unique and extraordinary person—I've heard nothing but good things about him. Even my Trojan spies that work inside the Greek camps—men that hate all Greeks—still tell me wonderful things about Patroclus. But now, Achilles, you're the only person alive who knows what it was like to really know Patroclus."

"Yes," Achilles said. "There will never be anyone else like him."

"Now, young man, let me tell you something that age has taught me: It will never get better. Despite what other say in supposed comfort, your hurt will never go away. It's how you must live until your own death."

"I've tried so hard to feel normal," Achilles said.

"You'll never feel normal again," Priam answered.

"Then why go on? Why don't we both kill each other tonight?"

"Because, my enemy, we're humans. You see, there are three kinds of life in this world: the Immortals, the animals, and the humans. The Immortals don't die. The animals do die, but they don't know that they'll die. Only humans die and know that they'll die. However, it's that knowledge that sets us apart. Without the fear of death, we would never know what courage feels like. Death turns chivalry into bravery, happiness into elation, and love into passion. The Immortals know nothing of courage, bravery, elation, and passion. It's death that gives us our intense emotions."

Achilles pondered long and hard. *Why haven't any of the Greeks said these things to me?* he wondered. *Do none of them have the sense to turn sympathy into truth?*

"You're telling me that my grief for Patroclus will never go away," Achilles said pensively. "That no matter what I do, and do not do, the grief stays forever. However, at the same time, it's the ability to feel grief that enables death to give me life."

"Yes," Priam said. "That's exactly what I'm saying. Grief is a privilege reserved for humans. Immortals, like animals, will never understand. Death is what makes life alive."

The fire in Achilles's soul finally extinguished itself. Calm descended upon him, and he breathed deeply. He got up from the table and stuck his head out of the tent. Briseis was sitting near, eating a meal by a fire.

"Briseis," Achilles said softly. "I'd like you to get some others and have Prince Hector's body taken to be washed and rubbed with oil. When he's ready, bring him back here and set him on a mule cart."

Briseis looked at him with surprise and stood. "Of course, Achilles." she said. "Right away."

"Also, please bring me some warm water and two pieces of meat. I'll wash and cook a dinner for my guest and me."

"Guest?" Briseis asked.

"Yes, a man, a friend, has snuck into my tent, and I'll prepare a meal for us."

Achilles went back inside and turned the torches so that more light came into the tent. Now, he could see the regal manner with which Priam sat. There was no doubt that he was a proud king.

Briseis returned with three men. She pointed to Hector, and the men took the dirty body. Hector's dead limbs dangled and were barely attached. Achilles stood in front of Priam so that he wouldn't see. Then Briseis returned with an animal skin of hot water. She bowed at Priam when she noticed him and helped Achilles wash.

I feel better. A lot better, Achilles realized.

He cooked a meal, and he and Priam shared it at the table. They talked of war and peace. Priam shared a few Trojan jokes about Agamemnon that Achilles laughed at loudly. They talked long into the night, long after the sounds of the outside camp faded into sleep.

Eventually, Achilles escorted Priam outside where the mule cart was waiting. Hector's body lay beneath a spotless white cloth. His face was perfect. *I'm glad about that,* Achilles thought.

Achilles helped Priam climb on the cart's bench. Then he ordered a group of four Myrmidons to make sure the cart had safe passage back to the gate of Troy. He watched Priam drive away and observed how noble the old king still appeared.

He went back inside the tent and called for Briseis.

"I'm very happy right now," Briseis said. "You look good. Your actions tonight have filled my soul with relief."

"I feel good," Achilles said. "I'm ready for a few days of solid sleep. We'll give the Trojans time to properly mourn Hector."

"I'll send your word to Agamemnon and the others. You'll sleep well. I'll make sure you're not disturbed."

"No, Briseis," Achilles said. "It's time for you to leave. Patroclus is dead and gone. There's no need for you to waste your life with me. He told me of your desire. I'd like you to choose a man among the Myrmidons whom you trust. Let him protect you on your journey. I'll give you enough gold to last for several lifetimes. Travel to the Hellespont and take a merchant ship to Egypt. You must get out of the Troad while you can. Learn all you can about healing. My only request is that, someday, you return to Greece and share your knowledge."

"I can't leave you," Briseis said. "Not now. There's more war to occur and wounds to heal. Patroclus would—"

"Patroclus isn't here anymore. That's why you must go. Thanks to the two of you, we have plenty of healers in the Greek camp. This isn't your fate anymore. Whatever ropes bound you to this war were completely severed by Patroclus. We're not your people. In fact, your people are gone. Go to Egypt and learn what you can. Make all people your people."

Briseis stood in silence for a long while and then said, "I'll do as you ask. This is a great gift that you give me. I won't squander it."

"Of all the people still alive in this world, you're the person I least expect to squander anything. I know I'm not always like other people. But I want you to know that I love you."

"I loved Patroclus and I love you," Briseis said. "I will see you again. I will never forget you."

Achilles watched her as she left the tent for the last time, with tears on her face.

Briseis, you're wrong and you're right, Achilles thought. *You'll never see me again. But you will remember me forever—everyone will. The prophesy that my mother told me by the sea is upon me. I won't return to Greece, and my name will live forever.*

Several days later…

THE FATES OF ACHILLES

ARIS TURNED OVER in bed and looked at Helen. She was peacefully asleep. Their relationship had improved since Aphrodite intervened, and he was glad they were happy again. *It's been ten years since I met her,* he thought. *Her face is a bit older, but even more beautiful. It's strange that all this pain has been caused by us being together. Yet nobody even seems to remember that anymore. We've been forgotten in all the strategy and politics. I wonder if Hector thought about us when he was fighting for his life. Did he resent me? Or had he forgotten as well? I suppose the war was never about Helen, and time has made that apparent.*

The Trojans expected that the fighting would resume, as the period of mourning for Hector had passed. Paris rolled over again, dreading the moment that some commander or another would knock on his door to wake him. He was heir to the throne of Troy and needed to act accordingly. He knew that many soldiers despised him because his weapon, the bow, was considered cowardly. *I can't help that I was raised shooting arrows at wolves,* he thought. *Why should I waste my talent thrashing about with a sword when I can kill many more Greeks from standing on a tower? Is it my fault that my weapon allows me to keep my distance from danger?*

Suddenly, he felt a hand shaking his arm. He jumped up, surprised that anyone was in the room when he hadn't heard the door open. When he fully came to his senses, he saw standing before him the same beautiful young nurse he'd seen after the duel with Menelaus.

"Aphrodite?" Paris asked.

"Yes," she answered.

Helen still slept comfortably and had not been wakened. Paris got up and stepped away from the bed. Aphrodite joined him by the window.

"I have important information for you," Aphrodite said. "Today, you'll stand on the wall and aim for Achilles."

"It's a waste of time and arrows," Paris replied. "I've seen him hit by arrows before, countless times, and they just bounce off his armor. I've even seen him get hit directly on his flesh, and still nothing seems to cause pain. And now with this new armor of his, I don't know that any of us will ever see the end of him."

"Listen to me," Aphrodite said. "His mother, the Immortal Thetis, gave birth to him in a sacred pool of water. The water surrounded his body. Except, his father pulled him out in order to save his life. He was saved by his father's grasp around his right ankle—which was never touched by the water. You can wound him with an arrow to the right ankle."

"With all due respect, Immortal Aphrodite, why didn't you share this news with Hector before he left for his death? Or, at least told me? I could have told him. Why didn't you tell us this ten years ago when Achilles conquered the Troad?"

"I don't owe any sort of explanation to you. But to protect my reputation as compassionate and loving, I'll tell you. Achilles's weakness is a human weakness. It didn't become apparent until he fully embraced his human side. The weakness didn't make itself known until recently. Now, go."

She walked out of the bedroom, leaving the door open. No sooner had she left than a soldier came to retrieve Paris. Helen woke and helped him dress in the royal armor that he wore well. He kissed her, grabbed his bow, and left his quarters.

In the courtyard, he encountered a group of four young servant women. They smiled, clung to each other, and giggled when he nodded to them. *It's nice to know that I still have that impact on women,* he thought. *Thank you, Aphrodite, for never taking away my beauty.*

He refused a horse and walked with the other soldiers through the city. The sun was shining, and it was already getting warm. He hoped that the afternoon would bring cool breezes to the streets of Troy. As they neared the gate, he heard the sounds of battle coming from the other side.

"The Greeks were up early this morning," a commander said to him.

"Anxious, I suppose," Paris replied. "It's been several days since they last made an attempt to breach the gate. How close are they?"

"They've gotten up to the wall, I'm afraid," the commander answered. "They broke our lines this morning."

"Is there any hope that we'll push them back and retake the Greek trench?"

"No, not now. Our focus is entirely on protecting the gate and the wall."

Paris thanked the man for the information and entered the bottom doorway of one of the two towers that supported the gate. He climbed up a spiral stone staircase and surveyed the situation from the top.

The Aegean Sea was as blue as he'd ever seen, and so calm that it appeared as a giant mirror. He saw the reflection of the remaining Greek ships. But the sounds of battle coming from right below him grabbed his attention. The Greeks had, indeed, gotten to the wall. He took his bow and shot a few arrows. Each arrow mortally wounded a Greek soldier.

Then he saw the only thing around that was as bright as the sun itself: the magnificent hair of Achilles flowing around his brilliant armor. Achilles was on a chariot, and Paris surmised that he must have just arrived at the battle. *Can I kill him before he kills? He looks different, somehow, from the last time I saw him. His face isn't as wrinkled with hate. Odd.*

He watched Achilles step off the chariot. Paris wasted no time. He thought about the words of Aphrodite and the face of his sleeping, beautiful Helen. He raised his bow, gently strung, and arrow, aimed, and released the string. It was the swiftest arrow he'd ever shot. He could tell he'd hit his mark even before the arrow fully cleared the bow.

Immediately, Achilles shouted with pain and fell to the ground. He raised his right leg, and Paris saw the arrow, which had penetrated the entire ankle. Achilles pulled at the arrow, but it wouldn't budge. Paris aimed again and shot another arrow directly into the side of Achilles's exposed throat. Blood began to spurt out in the rhythmic pulses of mighty Achilles's dying heart.

This night will be my night, Paris thought. *All of Troy will celebrate me and acclaim that I'm worthy of the thro-*

ne of Troy. King Priam will finally be proud of me, and Helen won't be ashamed to stay by my side. She'll dress in her finest and cling to me at dinner. The archers will finally receive the respect they deserve.

Before he left the tower he looked down at dying Achilles and out to the sea. The sky was still brilliantly blue, but the water was now strangely dark. Giant waves thrashed at the beach.

One moment later…

A HUMAN DIES

ACHILLES WAS GLAD for the second arrow because it stopped the pain of the first. The battle ceased immediately when he fell. *Now I must prepare for the end,* he thought. *Hurry, Greeks! Someone take my armor and body so that the Trojans don't get them.*

His eyes were open and he could still see surprisingly well. Odysseus was the first to come to him.

"Odysseus," Achilles said rather strongly, "take my armor and body."

"Of course," Odysseus said. "You're the greatest warrior that our people have ever known. We'll never allow you to be desecrated. I promise, tonight you'll be able to cross the river."

"You must secure the fleet immediately. The sea will become violent very soon. Move everything away from the beach."

"Don't worry about anything," Odysseus said. "I'll make sure that you and the Greek fleet are protected from harm."

"My ashes—gather them and put them into the same vase with Patroclus's ashes. Promise me. I must know that this will be done."

"I'll risk my own life and the lives of all my men to see that your last desire is fulfilled. Everyone will remember your name."

"I know they will."

After a period of mourning, in the Greek camp…

ODYSSEUS TELLS OF
TROY'S PROPHECIES

O DYSSEUS WATCHED OVER the funeral pyre and insisted that he himself gather the ashes of the corpse. Alone, he went to the mound where the vase of Patroclus had been deeply buried. He dug for hours and retrieved the vase. He poured Achilles in with Patroclus. He replaced the dirt and made sure that the mound was as serene as it deserved to be. When he left, out of the corner of his eye he saw a beautiful woman with black hair emerge from the sea. *She looks too dignified to be associated with humans, but much too sad to associate with those of Mount Olympus,* Odysseus thought.

The war was dormant for the next twelve days as the Greek kings proclaimed a series of games in honor of Achilles. Various contests of athletic skill were held, with winners receiving gifts.

During the middle of the games, a large fight broke out between Odysseus and Ajax the Greater. Both of these men wanted Achilles's armor. Odysseus believed he deserved it for fulfilling Achilles's last request and for being the most cunning of all the Greeks. Ajax believed he deserved the armor because he was the next best warrior among the Greeks, after Achilles. Agamemnon was given the privilege of deciding, and he chose Odysseus. Ajax the Greater could not live with this assault on his honor. He killed himself.

As the days of official mourning came to a close, Odysseus began to prepare for the inevitable upcoming return to battle. But first, he had some news to tell the other kings and commanders. He called for them all to gather inside Agamemnon's tent.

When Odysseus arrived at the assembly, he said to a soldier outside, "Go to my tent and bring my guest here. But don't let him enter until I call."

Odysseus entered and took a seat at the table. After twelve days of rest and feasting, the kings looked clean and healthy.

"We're here for Odysseus, as usual," Agamemnon said. "Tell us why."

"I've spent much time and gold to gather the news I'm about to tell you," Odysseus began. "I've discovered that Apollo himself has provided two conditions that must be met before Troy will fall."

"Prophesies?" Agamemnon asked. "Can they be trusted?"

"Yes, prophesies," Odysseus answered. "Due to the source of the information and the nature of the prophesies themselves, I firmly believe they're accurate. I can't think of any reason why these would have been fabricated."

"I don't understand," Diomedes said. "Are you saying that all we need to do is bring about these two conditions and Troy will fall?"

"Not exactly," Odysseus said. "But it's clear that we can't win until the conditions are met. We have no choice but to bring them about and then prepare to conquer the city in one final battle."

"Get on with it," Agamemnon said. "What are they?"

"The first is that the arrows of Heracles must be brought to Troy and used to kill the heir to the throne, which is now, of course, Paris."

"The arrows are lost," Nestor said. "The great archer Philoctetes had them, and he was lost at sea, along with the arrows."

"No," Ajax the Lesser said. "I believe that Philoctetes died of a festering wound and never told anyone where he'd hidden the arrows."

"You're both wrong," said Menelaus. "I was a good friend of Philoctetes. He was living on the island of Lemnos. When this war started, I sent word for him to join us. After a year, I hadn't heard a word from him. The only thing that could ever keep Philoctetes from battle is death. I believe he's dead and nobody knows what became of the arrows. In any regard, how can we accomplish this prophecy if the arrows don't exist?"

"They do exist," Odysseus said. "And here they are."

Odysseus stood, went to the tent door, and motioned for a man to come inside. A portly man, short and with a scraggly beard, walked into the tent. He carried a quiver of arrows. Menelaus immediately rose and embraced him.

"Philoctetes," Menelaus said, "where have you been?"

"On Lemnos," he said with a laugh, "this entire time. I'd been living in a village when I decided to spend the summer in the mountains. But I miscalculated the days and found myself trapped by deep snows. I had to spend all winter up there. Then, I decided that I might as well stay for the next summer since I was already up there. Anyway, I returned to the village, and they told me that a messenger had arrived, asking me to join in a war in Troy. Well, by that time it had been an entire year. I didn't think that you could possibly be at war for an entire year. So I grieved that I'd missed all the fun and went back to the mountains to live. I was there when Odysseus's men found me fifteen days ago. I came with the arrows as soon as I could."

"We have the arrows!" Agamemnon exclaimed.

"And," said Menelaus, "we have the best archer alive. Nobody is as precise with a bow as Philoctetes."

Odysseus watched while some of the others looked at Philoctetes in shock. He knew they were all wondering how this fat, jolly man could possibly be the legendary archer acclaimed throughout the world. *They'll learn that you don't need to be swift of feet or even strong of arm to have precise aim,* he thought. *You just need to be able to calm your entire mind and body at the right time.*

Agamemnon motioned for them all to sit. Menelaus poured some wine for Philoctetes.

"Now," said Nestor, "what is this second condition?"

This should be good, Odysseus thought. "This one is more difficult," he said. "The second condition is that the son of Achilles must be brought to Troy and put to work as a soldier who will kill the king himself."

Loud groans erupted from the men, followed by laughter. Odysseus saw that most of them were shaking their heads and rolling their eyes.

"I thought that the arrows of Heracles were impossible to get," said Diomedes. "But this second prophesy makes the first seem like child's play. How, my dear Odysseus, do we get a dead man who always chose another man when he was alive to have a son? Not even you, Odysseus, are that clever."

"We might as well sail home now," said Ajax the Lesser. "Apollo loves the Trojans and has created a condition that can't be met. This is true cleverness that only the Immortals can wield. It's actually brilliant when you think about it."

"It's an impossible prophesy," said Agamemnon. "It must be a trick to get us to leave. Have you thought of that, clever Odysseus?"

"Yes, I have thought of that. And, normally, I'd be inclined to believe that it's a ruse—except, I have information that proves it's a valid and accomplishable prophesy. I've taken care of it."

An enormous eruption of laughter occurred as Agamemnon said, "You're in over your head this time, Odysseus. Just admit it."

"You can all stop your doubts and laughter," Odysseus said. "Do you think Apollo is the only Immortal? Like I said before, I've taken care of it. I can't say, right now, how the solution will present itself because I can't trust that there are no spies listening. A spy would certainly intervene if he heard how I accomplished the task—a task that could be easily ruined. I can't possibly say at this time. But you must all trust me and know that soon, very soon, the son of Achilles will be among our soldiers."

It will be my finest hour, Odysseus thought. *At least until I tell them of the horse my slaves are building.*

The next morning, inside Troy…

THE FATE OF PARIS

ENEAS, PRINCE OF Dardania and of the royal family of Troy, loved Priam's palace. He'd practically grown up there. As a child, he'd often dreamed of what it would be like to be king of such a prosperous city like Troy. But, alas, he was very far down the order of succession. Until now.

I should have already been named heir to the throne, Aeneas thought. *After all, I grew up here and learned the ways of governing years before we even knew that Alexander or Paris or whatever his name is was still alive. I grew up beside Hector. But Priam chose Paris. Well, we'll see what time will bring.*

Aeneas, already in his armor, opened the door to Paris's quarters. Since Hector's death, Priam had tasked Aeneas with watching over Paris. He did this task dutifully because, worse than not getting the throne, would be rumors that he had killed to get the throne. It was not that he would not kill to get the throne. He just did not want there to be rumors that he had done it.

Helen and Paris were still asleep in their luxurious bed when Aeneas entered the room. *Whoever is king,* he mused, *Helen would make the most spectacular queen.* She was lying on top of Paris, her head resting on his chest. Aeneas rolled his eyes at how perfect the whole scene was. He reached over and shook Paris.

"Is it time already?" Paris asked. "How do we know they'll even fight today?"

"The time of Greek mourning is over," Aeneas said, annoyed. "They're going to make an advance on the gate. We have to move now while our men are fresh. We've decided to make a strong move to retake the Greek trench."

I'll do as Hector did, Aeneas thought. *I'll break through their wall and set fire to Greek ships. If I make myself more popular than Paris, I might have a chance to get Priam's attention.*

"Paris isn't going to be on the field, is he?" Helen asked as she sat up.

"No," Aeneas answered. "He can do a lot more with his bow on the tower than he can on the field. But we need to leave now. The army has been ready for some time."

Paris got up, and Aeneas watched as Helen helped him into the royal armor of Troy. Paris grabbed his bow and a quiver of arrows, then put on his helmet. Helen kissed him.

As they walked through the palace, and then the city itself, Aeneas watched how the young women swooned when Paris passed. He'd always been jealous of Hector, but Hector had merits that earned this envy. Aeneas didn't like being jealous of Paris. *Can I adequately protect him with all this jealousy building inside me?* he wondered. *We shall have to see.*

They climbed the tower by the gate and looked out over the scene of men preparing for battle. The Trojan army was amassing along the side of the city, ready to ambush the Greeks after the Trojan archers had cleared the plain. Aeneas saw the Greeks assembling in front of their trench.

They did not dare advance with the Trojan archers perched strategically on the walls.

Suddenly, from among the Greek lines, a chariot moved quickly forward. Menelaus was driving it in full armor. However, it was the passenger who grabbed Aeneas's attention. The passenger was a large man wearing no armor. He leaned against the side of the chariot, seemingly without a care in the world.

"Who is that man?" Paris asked. "Some sort of mascot?"

"I have no idea," Aeneas answered. "He doesn't look like much of a soldier, does he?"

They both moved to the edge of the tower to get a clearer look. The chariot came right underneath them. Then Aeneas saw the large man take an arrow and place it on his bow. The man lifted the bow slightly and shot the arrow without even seeming to aim. The arrow flew up to the tower, grazed Paris's exposed forearm, and landed on the stone floor. Aeneas and Paris both laughed.

"You missed!" Aeneas shouted down to the chariot with a loud laugh.

"No, I didn't!" the rotund man shouted back.

The chariot raced away as Paris and Aeneas looked at each other with humor. Aeneas saw all the Trojan archers leaning over the side of the wall, pointing and laughing at the fat man in the chariot.

"Did the arrow wound you at all?" Aeneas asked.

"Hardly," Paris said. "Look, it made the smallest scratch I've ever had in my life. I won't be winning any sympathy with this wound."

Then, the Greek lines began to advance. The archers gathered their wits and attempted to keep the Greeks as far back as possible. Aeneas gave the signal to prepare the Trojan army to advance. However, Aeneas noticed that Paris's aim was dismal. He wasn't hitting any Greek soldier, and his arrows flew into the ground itself. *Whatever I think of Paris, he's never off with his bow. Something's wrong.*

"Paris, are you okay?" Aeneas said.

"I'm not sure," Paris answered. "I feel just a bit queasy. I think I'll go down and get some water."

Aeneas watched him descend the stairs, then he decided that he'd better follow in case Paris needed help. The arrow that the large man shot was still lying on the stones. Aeneas picked it up, noticed that it was still perfect, and placed it into Paris's quiver. He brought the quiver with him.

When he reached the bottom of the tower, he saw that Paris was crumpled against the side of it, barely able to stand on his feet. Aeneas grabbed him, and the two started walking up into the city.

"I think I need to go to the palace," Paris said. "I don't feel good at all. Something is terribly wrong."

Aeneas noticed that Paris was getting hot and turning red all over. He motioned to a soldier and got a mule cart to drive them up the hill of Troy.

When they arrived at the palace, Aeneas was astounded at how quickly Paris had deteriorated. He was breathing heavily and complaining that his helmet was too tight. Aeneas threw off the helmet. Paris barely looked like Paris. His head was swollen and his hair had even begun to fall out. Aeneas yelled for help. A group of servants carried Paris into the palace and directly to his bed.

Helen became catatonic when she saw Paris. Aeneas couldn't handle her screams and called for her handmaidens to take care of her. Paris was fading fast. He began to convulse on the bed. Priam, Hecuba, and the priest of Apollo ran into the room. Everyone crowded around the dying prince.

"What happened?" Priam asked.

"Nothing, really," Aeneas answered. "He was barely scratched by an arrow shot from a Greek."

The priest of Apollo examined Paris. Then, Paris became completely rigid for a few moments. He made a slight gurgling sound while his body relaxed and softened. He was still.

"He has died," the priest said. "Where's the arrow?"

"In his quiver," Aeneas said. "It's back on the cart."

The priest sent for the quiver but gave explicit instructions to the servant not to touch any of the arrows. Hecuba started wailing, which made Helen wail louder. The noise in the stone room was deafening. *I can't concentrate on anything with these women going on like this,* Aeneas thought.

The quiver arrived and Aeneas pointed to the perfect arrow. The priest slowly and deliberately removed the arrow. He was extremely careful not to touch the finely crafted point. The priest walked over to the lamp and placed the arrowhead directly into the fire. A normal arrow would have merely grown hot, but Aeneas watched as this arrow burst into a brilliant blue flame.

"As I suspected," the priest of Apollo said. "This arrow was dipped into the blood of the Hydra. This arrow belonged to Heracles. Prince Alexander died of poison."

"No," said Priam as he crumpled onto a chair. "It cannot be."

"Yes," the priest said. "There's no doubt."

"Did the man who shot this arrow specifically aim for Prince Paris?" Priam asked.

"I believe so," Aeneas said. "But he was so clever that he hardly aimed at all. But, yes, I would say that his target was Paris."

"This means that the Greeks know about our prophesy," Priam said. "An arrow of Heracles has killed the heir of Troy."

"But the second prophesy can nev—" the priest began.

"I don't care!" Priam shouted. "They know the prophesies, and they will make the second one come true. We must be very careful."

What are they talking about? Aeneas wondered. *Prophesies are tricky things to be dealing with. But, with Paris dead, is this my time?*

Priam walked up to Aeneas and took his hands. There was a determined look in his eyes that Aeneas had not seen before.

"Aeneas," Priam said, "you are the heir of Troy. Go to the commanders. Call off all fighting. Every Trojan is to come inside the city, and the gate is to be sealed. We'll live on the stores that have been restocked. No one enters the city and no one leaves. This is how we'll live until the Greeks leave."

Finally, I'm heir to the throne of Troy, Aeneas thought. *Now we must win this war.*

A few days later…

ODYSSEUS HAS A SOLUTION

A GAMEMNON PREPARED TO enter his tent. He moved slowly and slumped against a tent pole. *I've never felt like this in my entire life,* he thought. *My body and my spirit are both ill. This is going to be incredibly demeaning, but it has to be done.*

Earlier, he'd called for a war council. When he finally entered the tent, he saw that all were present except for Odysseus. *He's never late, but it's better he doesn't have to hear this anyway.*

"Kings of Greece and other commanders," Agamemnon said, "I've made a decision about the war. I'm not looking for debate over this, but I am seeking understanding."

The leaders shifted on their chairs. Agamemnon studied their faces. He couldn't tell who would be easy to convince and who would argue with him.

"Priam has locked the city of Troy once again," Agamemnon began. "We've been informed that they were able to replenish most of their stores over the last few moons when the battle was raging. We don't expect that they'll fall on their own for at least another few years. Probably four or more."

Some of the men groaned loudly in the tent. A few laughed.

"I've been torn between two options: should we give everything we have to breach the gate, or should we just go home? I've come to the conclusion that it's futile to attack the city. It's rumored that the walls and the gate were built by Apollo himself. I now concede that it's probably true. And so, as much as it pains me to say this, we'll board our ships and sail for Greece."

"No!" Diomedes shouted. "How will we face our people? Our wives? Gone for ten years and nothing to show for it. They'll disown us."

"Don't you think I've considered that?" Agamemnon said. "You must know that I'm the last among us to want to face his wife. I'm married to Clytemnestra, remember? Compared to her, you're all married to daisies and daffodils. Clytemnestra will destroy me over this. But I don't see that there's any way out of war without retreat to Greece."

"Men," Nestor said strongly, "allow me to speak in favor of Agamemnon and his plan to retreat. We must not forget about the second prophesy. Even if we get into Troy, the city won't fall unless we have the son of Achilles. To attack with that hanging over our heads would cause thousands of needless deaths. Agamemnon is prudent and has courage enough to do the right thing. I, for one, would—"

"What's all this talk of retreating?" Odysseus said as he entered the tent. "I told you all to trust me, especially about the prophesy. Now, here I come with a solution to all your problems, and you've already decided to give up without me. I should just take my solution and go back to—"

"Sit and talk," Agamemnon said. "Nobody can stop you anyway."

Odysseus opened the tent flap wider and revealed that a young boy was standing next to him. He pushed the boy into the tent. Odysseus guided the boy into the light of a lamp. The room erupted in gasps as the boy's brilliant hair glowed like the sun.

Odysseus doesn't disappoint! Agamemnon thought. *Perhaps I won't have to face Clytemnestra after all.*

"How can this be?" Ajax the Lesser asked. "He looks like a miniature Achilles. What sorcery have you conjured up, Odysseus?"

"No sorcery," Odysseus said. "This child was begat the same way we all were, although, maybe with a little less pleasure. Please, boy, introduce yourself to the war council as I prepared you to do."

"Fellow leaders of Greece," the boy said, "I'm Neoptolemus. I'm ten years old. My mother is Deidamia, princess of Skyros, and my father is the great Achilles. Both my grandfathers are kings, and my grandmother is the Immortal Thetis, relative of Poseidon."

"Thank you, Neoptolemus," Odysseus said. "Now, go and practice throwing spears with my men while I talk about you in here with these astonished-looking fellows."

The boy nodded and left.

What a story this should be! Agamemnon thought. *Odysseus will surely want much gold for this—and he deserves it!*

"Ten years ago," Odysseus said, "Diomedes and I went to the island of Skyros, where Thetis had hidden Achilles. Achilles was in disguise as a dancing princess, one of the king's many daughters."

"We've all heard the story many times," Menelaus said. "It's one of your favorites to tell around the fire."

"But," said Odysseus, "I've never told the ending until now. Achilles and Patroclus left with Diomedes to return to the Myrmidon camp. There was much to do to prepare them to march. However, I lagged behind at the palace of Lycomedes. Many of you know that I never leave a location until I've gotten some of the servants drunk—it's how you can get the best, and most truthful, news. I wanted to know if Lycomedes had a secret army on Skyros that we could use. I found a married servant couple. The man was the bedchamber servant of the king, and the woman was a handmaiden in the service of the daughters. I learned that Lycomedes's oldest daughter was a beautiful woman named Deidamia.

"One night, the servants told me, Deidamia walked into a room and caught a servant man in bed with one of the princesses. Deidamia was about to scream when they stopped her. It turned out that the servant was actually Patroclus in disguise. But Deidamia was even more astonished to discover that the princess was, in reality, the famous warrior Achilles.

"The handmaiden told me that Deidamia wasn't unknown to men. Also, the princess enjoyed being this way. Deidamia threatened to expose the men and have Patroclus executed unless Achilles shared a bed with her. She demanded that the famous warrior Achilles make love to her, or Patroclus would pay the price.

"I don't have any details about what exactly occurred, or how the men reacted to it. But I kept my flow of information open with the servants. Using messengers and several pieces of gold, I discovered that nine moons after Diomedes and I took Achilles away from Skyros, Deidamia gave birth to a son. Now, we've all seen this boy. Is there any doubt as to the identity of his father?"

"No doubt," said Nestor. "Well done, Odysseus. But how is Neoptolemus's demeanor? Can we put someone so young to the task of killing the king of Troy, as the prophesy requires? He's only ten years of age."

"He looks exactly like Achilles," Odysseus said. "But, miraculously, his demeanor is more like that of Patroclus. He's a nice and respectful young man. However, you should also know that King Lycomedes sent him to be trained in Phythia. He can handle a spear, and a bit of a sword. He need not fight alone. I'll always be next to him."

"Clever Odysseus," Agamemnon said. "I give you great honor for solving one problem. But there's another. Tell me, what does your brilliant mind see about getting through the gate?"

"I've been working on that for over a year," Odysseus said. "The plans are ready. Now, men, gather in tight around me. If my plan stays secret, we'll conquer Troy. However, if even the slightest of details is leaked, we'll all die a terrible and painful death. Now is the time to realize that our loyalty to one another is our greatest weapon."

The war has moved from being about Menelaus to being about Achilles to now being about Odysseus, Agamemnon thought. *Where am I in any of this?*

Two days later...

THE GIFT HORSE

.

"**I**T CANNOT BE!" Priam shouted as he jumped out of bed.

All around the palace, so many people were yelling about the Greeks that the building shook with excitement. He ran into Aeneas in a corridor. Neither of them was dressed to receive each other, and neither of them cared.

"Is it true?" Priam asked.

"I have no idea," Aeneas replied.

They walked as fast as Priam in his old age could handle, through the great hall, and up the spiral staircase. At the top, they looked out over what used to be a war-torn plain.

It's true! Priam thought.

The Greek trench was almost entirely filled with discarded items. Their wall contained several large gaps where sections of it had been pulled down. The plain was completely bare. However, beyond that, the beach was strewn with dead Greek bodies. Priam looked to the sea and saw only water—no Greek ships spoiled the view. *I haven't seen this open water for ten years!* he thought.

Then his attention came to something on the beach. Aeneas pointed it out as well. It was so large that even from their distance they could see that it was a horse made of wood.

"We'll investigate," said Priam. "Call my advisors and a guard. And get the priest of Apollo."

"I'll investigate," Aeneas said.

"No," Priam answered. "I haven't been outside the city for over ten years. I'm going with you."

They dressed, mounted horses, and galloped to the gate as it slowly opened. The people of Troy looked at them as they passed, but everyone remained silent. *No one is sure what to do. They're waiting for me*, Priam thought.

The horses crossed the Greek trench using some planks, then walked through the openings in the wall. On the beach, the men dismounted.

"The bodies are rough," said the priest of Apollo. "Too far gone to know what occurred. But they left without giving the dead proper funerals. This is very odd. Perhaps some kind of plague?"

Priam walked slowly to the giant horse. It was finely crafted of new wood gathered from the nearby forest. Its giant legs sat on top of wooden platforms that rested on the sand. He touched it, then knocked on it. It was hollow and silent.

"What is it?" Aeneas asked.

"The horse is the symbol of Troy," Priam said. "Is it some kind of peace offering?"

"Have you considered that there could be Greeks hiding inside the horse?" Aeneas said. "Perhaps they'll jump out and attack."

"Without ships or an army?" Priam said. "What would be the point?"

"They knew you'd come down," Aeneas said. "It could be a way to lure you to your death."

Priam ordered his commanders to search the entire area. He instructed them to make sure to search for any sign that Greek ships were still near the shore. He also sent for Helen.

When Helen arrived, Priam said to her, "We think that there may be Greeks inside. If there are, there's a good chance that Menelaus is with them—he'd never voluntarily leave without you. Go to the horse and call to him. Try to lure him out."

Helen walked to the horse and yelled, "Menelaus! Menelaus! It's me, your wife, Helen. We know that you Greeks are in there. Let's not spill any more blood. Come out of the horse, and I'll go with you, peacefully, back to Sparta. Paris is dead. Your war has killed him. There's no argument between us now. I'm ready to be the queen of Sparta once again."

The Trojans stood as silent as any group of people could possibly be. Nothing came from the horse, no man and no sound.

"Agamemnon!" Helen shouted. "I've had word from my sister and your wife, Queen Clytemnestra. She's glad that you've been absent so long. She claims that you're such a lousy lover that your kids are not even your kids."

Still, no sound or movement.

Helen, I didn't know you had it in you, Priam thought. *Have you finally chosen a side? Maybe. However, no man could have stayed silent and still while hearing these things. I believe the horse to be empty.*

Helen went back into Troy, and the men sat on the beach just in front of the horse.

"Should we burn it?" Aeneas asked.

"Be careful," the priest of Apollo said. "Perhaps the Greeks wanted to honor us. Apollo is our patron. If we burn the horse, we risk insulting Apollo. We should leave it here on the beach."

After they spent a few minutes contemplating, a chariot came racing in their direction from the woods on the side of Troy opposite the Hellespont. The chariot kicked up sand as it quickly advanced. A Trojan soldier stood on the chariot, and there was a severely wounded man lying in the back. Aeneas, Priam, and the others gathered around the chariot when it stopped.

The wounded man was a mass of blood and flesh. He looked practically more dead than alive. He wore a cloak that, even though torn and shabby, was recognizable.

"He's Lyrnessian," Priam said. "I can tell by the torn cloak." Then he turned to the wounded man and asked, "Can you speak?"

"Yes," the man replied. "I have strength left in me, but I need help."

"We'll help," Priam said. "I give you my word as king of Troy. Do you know anything about how the Greeks left our shore?"

"Yes," the man replied. "They thought I was dead."

"You're Lyrnessian?" Priam said. "Tell us what you know."

"Yes, I'm Lyrnessian. I was captured with several others of my kind by Achilles when he sacked my city. We were given to the Greek Odysseus and served him."

"I heard a rumor," Aeneas said, "that Odysseus had a great argument with some Lyrnessian slaves."

"I heard the same," said the priest of Apollo.

"We fought over this great wood horse that you see. My Lyrnessian brothers and I were tasked with building the horse. It took a moon. We worked in the woods."

"Before you continue," Aeneas said, "are you loyal to Troy or Greece?"

"Honestly, I was loyal to neither. But the Greeks defiled a Lyrnessian priestess named Chryseis. That's when we all became loyal to Troy."

"Go on," Aeneas said.

"There was a plague caused by Apollo shortly after Achilles died. That's why there are so many dead on the beach. Then Odysseus heard from Athena—she loves the Greeks. Athena instructed Agamemnon to retreat to Greece. But, Agamemnon was worried about bringing the plague back with him. Athena came up with the idea of constructing a great tribute to the city of Troy. Apollo, who so loves Troy, would see the tribute and end the plague."

"That explains the horse," Priam said. "But why were you fighting with Odysseus and how did you get into the state you're in?"

"My Lyrnessian friends and I accidentally heard a critical piece of information. Odysseus didn't know that we were working in the trees when he was talking to Agamemnon. It seems that Athena had a warning for Odysseus. She said that if, somehow, the great horse was brought into Troy, paraded up the streets, and placed in front of her temple by the Trojan palace, then she would have no choice but to switch allegiance and protect Troy. In that case, Troy would never, ever, fall. This is why Odysseus constructed the horse so that it's too tall to fit within the gate to the city."

"And he was angry that you knew about Athena's warning?" Priam asked.

"He was furious. He heard us in the trees. He wanted to kill us right then, but we were the only ones who could finish the horse in time. We tried to escape and caused quite an uproar in the camp. However, there's no winning against Odysseus. In the end, we finished the horse, and he killed all the Lyrnessians. He thought he'd killed me. But I played dead for some time then crawled into the woods, where your soldier found me."

"Sound the trumpets!" Priam yelled. "Tell the city that the war is over. Tell them—"

"Is this wise?" Aeneas interrupted.

"I'm king!" Priam shouted. "I'm, finally, a true king of a true city. Tell the city to cheer, drink wine, eat, and make Trojan babies. Task some men to tear down the stone arches over the gates so that the horse may fit. Get the army to bring large logs for the horse. We'll roll it up to the temple of Athena and celebrate our victory. You've heard this man—whom I trust! Athena will protect Troy for all time!"

At the same time...

THE SACKING OF TROY

INSIDE THE HORSE, Diomedes was last in and first out. Consequently, he sat on top of the concealed trapdoor under the horse's belly. When Agamemnon closed the door before he left with the ships, Diomedes complimented Odysseus's slaves. It was completely dark inside, not a single point of light penetrated the wood. The leaders were near the door. The child Neoptolemus sat between Diomedes and Odysseus. Then came Menelaus and Ajax the Lesser. Surrounding them, nineteen Myrmidons filled every available space.

The biggest fear inside the horse was that the Trojans would set the sculpture on fire. That was precisely why they chose the well-trained Myrmidons. Odysseus spent hours preparing Neoptolemus. If it hadn't been required that the kid get as close to the palace as possible, they never would have taken the risk. However, if any kid had the right temperament to be calm under pressure, it was Neoptolemus.

After the door closed, there came an unending silence. Odysseus had instructed that if any man made even the slightest sound, the man next to him was supposed to, quietly, kill him. But worse than the silence was the sound of Trojan voices discussing what to do with the horse. Diomedes felt as if his heart was outside his body, especially anytime they spoke of fire.

He heard them talking about a plague of Apollo. But Diomedes knew that none of the dead men on the beach died of illness. Over the years, it was inevitable that some of the soldiers would commit crimes against each other, mostly due to gambling or jealousy. The worst criminals were put into a special unit under Odysseus. He used them for activities that came with a higher-than-normal chance of casualties. When it came time for the fake plague, Odysseus and Philoctetes calmly scratched each man with one of Heracles's Hydra arrows.

Diomedes could feel the tension inside the horse when they heard the voice of Helen. He wondered if Menelaus might take the bait. But to his credit, he remained still and absolutely silent. Diomedes was glad that Agamemnon had the task of organizing the fleet. He did not think Agamemnon would have been as calm when Helen taunted him.

It had been Diomedes's job to recruit a man to play the wounded Lyrnessian soldier. He found a soldier famous in the Greek camp for his storytelling around the fire. Diomedes actually liked this man and wasn't looking forward to having to beat him severely enough to cause terrible wounds. But Odysseus gave him the idea of just pushing the man in front of a speeding chariot. So that's what he did. They paid the storyteller handsomely, and, inside the horse, Diomedes felt they had gotten their gold's worth when the man did a spectacular job. The real Lyrnessians had, indeed, been killed out of fear that they might spoil the secret.

To Diomedes, the best sound in the world was the clang of hammers and chisels knocking apart the stone arches over the gate. He reached over Neoptolemus and gave Odysseus a pat on the back when they heard thousands of Trojans cheering as the giant horse strained forward and slanted upward.

He began to think that the city would never stop celebrating. After the horse came to a stop, hours of revelry began. It was impossible to tell one voice from another among all the chaos. Diomedes liked to think that Priam and Hecuba were standing right under him, neither one knowing they were drinking their last wine.

At last, the noise of frolicking died down. Then came silence. Diomedes was to wait until Odysseus gave him a signal. The wait was unbearable, but Diomedes knew that Odysseus wasn't going to make an impatient mistake. Finally, Odysseus reached over Neoptolemus and tightly squeezed Diomedes's arm.

Diomedes carefully shifted his weight and unlatched the door. He held on to it as it swung down and opened. A rope ladder had been securely attached to the inside, and he silently let the ladder drop, bit by bit. He climbed down. It was dark with only a few torches lit in front of the temple of Athena. His eyes adjusted quickly. He glanced at Priam's palace, next to the temple, and saw no movement. The square had been abandoned.

He helped Neoptolemus down. Odysseus jumped out, picked up Neoptolemus, and ran off toward the palace. Menelaus climbed down, nodded to Diomedes, and took off after Odysseus. Ajax the Lesser descended, quickly followed by the well-trained Myrmidons. Diomedes, Ajax, and half the Myrmidons started running through the city. Down and down they continued. Nothing stirred in any of the buildings or homes. Occasionally, they came upon citizens lying in the street, who stirred when they passed. The Myrmidons quickly slit their throats and continued running.

When they got to the great gate, Ajax the Lesser and the Myrmidons silently killed all Trojans near it. Diomedes grabbed a torch from the wall and bounded up the stone steps to the top of one of the gate's towers. He heard the gate open, and he waved the torch wildly over his head. From this vantage, he could see how the Trojans had destroyed the stone arches that had previously secured the gate.

He looked over the plain and the beach. He didn't see any movement and questioned whether Agamemnon had accomplished his task. In his defense, Agamemnon had the more difficult assignment. He needed to command hundreds of ships. They were required to sail far enough that they wouldn't be seen but close enough to return to the shore in time to unload. They were supposed to anchor on the far side of the nearby island of Imbrose, but Diomedes had no way of knowing if that had actually occurred.

Finally, he saw dark shapes running across the plain. First hundreds, then thousands of men ran in the dark. He watched them silently run through the gate. Then, as the soldiers splintered off into the city, the screams started. They were followed by flames. Diomedes stood on the tower and watched the unbelievable sight of hundreds of fires appearing out of the darkness and getting higher and higher.

◉ ◉ ◉

Priam was awakened by the sound of a screaming woman. It took him less than an instant to realize that he'd been outsmarted by the Greeks. They'd used his devotion to the Immortals against him, and the city would be obliterated. Strangely, he found peace in the inevitability of it all.

He didn't know where Hecuba had decided to sleep and didn't want to waste time looking for her. He got up and didn't bother changing out of the clothes that he'd been sleeping in. As he walked out of the room, he noticed a wreath made of laurel branches sitting on a chair. Hecuba had made it for him the night before to wear as a reminder to all that he was king. Priam grabbed the wreath and put it on his head.

Troy was gone—there was nothing to be done about that. But there might still be a chance to save the culture. He was on a mission to find the one person who could possibly secure a future for the Trojan people. He found him in the great hall: Aeneas, in full royal amor.

"Priam!" Aeneas shouted as he ran to him. "We need to get you to safety. I'll form a guard."

"No," Priam said. "The time for fighting is well over. Take off your armor, Aeneas. You must dress in rags. There will be chaos as the city burns. Many Trojans will be able to escape among all the commotion. You need to get yourself out of the city. Eventually, you must gather what's left of the Trojans and lead them to a new place. Take them far away to a country that has no great city. There, find a river and build the beginnings of a great city."

Aeneas didn't say anything. He just nodded. Priam had tears in his eyes. He grabbed Aeneas's helmet off his head and threw it to the floor. He took the laurel wreath from his own head and placed it on Aeneas.

"This will be the crown of Troy," Priam said. "It was made by Queen Hecuba herself. Wear it until a future generation can craft something better."

Quickly, Aeneas threw off the rest of his armor. Priam watched with little emotion as Aeneas ran out of sight.

Then he saw the first Greek barge through the door and into the great hall. It was Odysseus.

◎ ◎ ◎

Odysseus ran into the great hall, followed closely by Neoptolemus. He was wondering whom he would have to kill in order to find out where the king was, but then he saw Priam standing in the middle of the room. There was no mistake to Odysseus. Only the true king of Troy could look so regal in such disheveled clothing.

"Priam?" Odysseus asked as he approached.

"Yes," Priam replied. "Can there be a negotiation? Can lives be saved?"

"No," Odysseus said. "Not after ten years. We owe this to our loved ones back in Greece."

"Of course," Priam said.

Neoptolemus came around Odysseus. Priam looked at him with wide eyes. Odysseus enjoyed this moment.

"So, it's true then," Priam said. "There's no mistaking that this is the son of Achilles."

"No mistaking," Odysseus said.

Odysseus handed a dagger to Neoptolemus. The boy took it and stood directly in front of Priam.

"Go ahead," Odysseus said. "It's time for you to avenge your father's death and bring about the end of Troy."

Neoptolemus didn't speak. He pushed the dagger into Priam's stomach. The old man fell to the floor. Then, Odysseus helped Neoptolemus slit the throat of the king of Troy.

By now, Myrmidon soldiers were streaming into the great hall. Odysseus grabbed one and gave him the task of seeing Neoptolemus safely back to a Greek ship. Then

Odysseus continued on his journey. He had one more task to complete.

He ran through the palace shouting at each servant he met to tell him the location of Hector's wife. Whatever their response, he killed them and moved on until he got credible information. Eventually, he found Andromache and the small Astyanax. They were standing, alone, on the top of a tower that overlooked the entire city. Odysseus surmised that from this vantage, Priam could have probably seen all the way to the sea.

Andromache fell to her knees and covered Astyanax.

"Princess Andromache," Odysseus said, "you know what I have to do. You protect an asset too important to survive. You protect the blood of Priam and Hector."

"You don't have to do anything," Andromache replied harshly. "He's a small child. Look around! The only thing he'll ever have claim to is a pile of ashes. Aeneas is heir to the throne, or whatever is left of one. Go and find him."

Odysseus realized that he did, as Andromache said, have a choice. But he couldn't deny that he had a deep desire to see Hector's son die.

He walked over and shoved Andromache aside. She screamed as Astyanax rolled out of her grasp. Then, before Odysseus could retrieve his sword, Andromache grabbed it from Odysseus's belt. She threw it over the side of the tower. Odysseus shrugged, grabbed Astyanax, walked over to the edge, and hurled the child down at the ground.

The blood of Troy splattered on the stones below.

◎ ◎ ◎

As had all the rest of the royal family, Helen woke to screams. But unlike them, she rose, washed herself, and dressed in her finest clothes. She adorned herself with jewelry and fixed her hair. Then she sat on a chair and waited.

The screaming was almost as unbearable as the smell of smoke that started to come in through the windows. She spent a great deal of time looking at the bed where Paris and she had enjoyed countless moments together.

Eventually the inevitable happened. The door to her chamber opened, and Menelaus calmly walked through. He appeared older to Helen, but in many ways, better. He seemed wiser and more dignified.

"I don't know what to say to you," Menelaus said.

"I don't know either," said Helen.

"I'm tired and just want to go home."

"I don't know where my home is," Helen replied.

"You'll find that out as time goes on," Menelaus said. "Do you want to come with me, or disappear into the city?"

"Decisions," Helen said. "Always decisions! I'm tired of them."

"Then come with me."

Menelaus grabbed her arm and lifted her to her feet. She began the most difficult walk of her life. Chaos was everywhere. Only someone with the recognizable stature of Menelaus could possibly have walked through the streets unharmed. Greeks and Trojans paused and stared when they passed. Helen could only imagine what they were thinking.

Death was all around. And all around the death was rape and torture. Greeks poured wine on each other. They wore the jewelry taken off dead Trojan women and Trojan women who wished they were dead.

Menelaus and Helen walked out the gate of Troy and crossed the plain. He carried her over the bodies on the beach. He put her in a small boat and instructed that she be taken to his ship.

She didn't sleep. When the sun came up, she looked over the deck of Menelaus's ship. Greeks were streaming back to the fleet, carrying the spoils of Troy. The city itself remained a mountain of fire and smoke. Nothing was recognizable, not even the great walls. Every structure had been reinforced and built around wood. When the wood burned, the structure fell.

The Greek leaders sat on chairs that had been placed on the beach. They sat in a row: Ajax the Lesser, Nestor, Diomedes, Odysseus, Menelaus, and Agamemnon. Helen wondered if they were happy with their triumph, or sad from all that had occurred to lead them to this place. She wondered if she herself would ever be really happy or really sad again. In the numbness she felt in sight of the great city on fire, she forced herself to feel nothing.

◎ ◎ ◎

Nestor sat on a chair next to the other victorious commanders of Greece. He realized that this was his last battle, his last war. Surprisingly, he wasn't sad about this. Nestor looked forward to returning home to his kingdom and family.

Still, it was quite bitter-sweet to watch Troy burn to the ground. The screams and shouts had stopped when the sun rose, but the flames were just as high. He wondered if they'd made a mistake burning everything instead of allowing the city to remain.

"Well, brother," Agamemnon said as he broke the silence, "it's all over. You have your wife back."

"And you have your gold," Menelaus said.

"This isn't entirely on me, you know," Agamemnon said. "There is a whole group of us that will enjoy the spoils and a Hellespont free of tariffs. I also haven't noticed you turning away any riches. The soldiers carry just as much treasure onto Spartan ships as they do to the others."

"I'm tired of hearing you talk, Agamemnon," Nestor said. "It's been ten years. Give Menelaus a break—give us all a break. I'm older than both of you brothers put together. What's done is done. That's probably the only truth that we know. What's done is done. It's possible to enjoy the gold and the satisfaction of Helen. It's possible to rejoice in the Hellespont and feel glad to have your family back together. But now it's time to listen to an old man. Here's what I'd like to tell you more than anything else: it's possible to celebrate victory and feel despair for all the Trojan suffering."

Nobody said anything else. Nestor listened to the sounds of the fire before him and the crashing waves of the Aegean behind him. He turned to his right. Far in the distance, the sun was lighting the mound of Achilles and Patroclus. He thought about all that had occurred over the past years. He shrugged and smiled.

As he watched the place where Achilles and Patroclus were buried, Nestor began to think about his own death. He didn't know how many mornings he had left, but he knew that time was against him. He thought about himself being ashes in a vase, just as those of Achilles and Patroclus were buried beneath the mound. Then, he pushed that thought out of his mind as he realized he was happy to be returning home.

CONCLUSION

L EAVING WAR CAN sometimes be as difficult as being in one. Men who defined themselves by fighting
alongside Achilles were now back to plowing fields.
For ten years, these men had grown accustomed to a certain type of lifestyle. After the war, every day would be
ordinary. Still, as sad as it was to leave close friendships
behind, it must have been nice to come home.

The Immortals were not pleased with how ruthlessly
the Greeks sacked Troy. Consequently, many of them were
hindered by Poseidon on their return voyage. Nestor and
Diomedes were among the only Greeks to arrive home just
four days after they left Troy. Nestor returned to Pylos,
where he raised his remaining sons. Diomedes returned to
Argos and had many adventures.

Odysseus's journey back to Ithaca from Troy is well do-
cumented and deserves its own book. The Immortals pu-
nished him severely for throwing the child Astyanax from
the tallest tower in Troy. He required ten more years of
sailing, fighting, plotting, loving, and all manner of turmoil before he finally returned to Ithaca.

Achilles had two fates. He chose to go to Troy, die, and
be remembered forever. Perhaps it's most fitting that his
son, Neoptolemus, lived the other fate. Neoptolemus lived

a long and happy life in Greece. But, today, hardly anyone remembers that Achilles even had a son.

Briseis traveled to Egypt and found herself at the great city of Memphis. There she spent several years learning from the physicians and the embalmers. She returned to Greece. Briseis used her great wealth, attained from Achilles, to open a school for healers in Athens. She never married again.

Hector's wife, Andromache, lived the life that Hector feared. She died after many years of serving as a slave in Greece.

Agamemnon returned to Mycenae with most of the spoils of Troy. However, Clytemnestra never forgave him for sacrificing Iphigenia. Clytemnestra killed Agamemnon and installed her lover as king of Mycenae. Then, Clytemnestra herself was killed by her son Orestes.

On their way across the Aegean, Menelaus and Helen were captured by an Egyptian ship. They spent eight years as the pharaoh's prisoners in the cult city of Akhetaten. Eventually, they returned to Sparta. Ironically, they were among the only couples in the saga to live a long and happy life together.

Aeneas did successfully lead a large group of Trojans out of the Troad. They traveled far and established a city on a river—just as Priam had instructed. Aeneas kept the laurel wreath crown, and it became the symbol of his new city. Eventually, that city obtained a name: Rome. Generations later, a direct descendant of Aeneas was named Julius Caesar. Somewhere in the afterlife, Priam and Hector must have been delighted that their kin became the most powerful nation on earth.

The land that contained the great city of Troy, now modern-day Turkey, saw similar violent activity during World

War I. The Battle of Gallipoli was every bit as bloody as the Trojan War. Over a hundred thousand soldiers from many nations lost their lives.

The Hellespont is now called the Dardanelles, and modern cruise ships sail the waters where one thousand ships once went to get Helen. On March 18, 2022, the Çanakkale Bridge opened across the Dardanelles. It's the longest suspension bridge in the world. For the first time in history, people can cross these waters without a sailing vessel. Unfortunately, the idea of a tariff did not die with the Trojans. It costs fifteen Euros to cross the Hellespont—each way.

Tourists on the cruise ships visit the archeological site that many scholars believe is the city that inspired the history of the Trojan War. There is even a giant wooden horse in the parking lot. And lots of souvenirs.

Lastly, people still visit Achilles's tumulus, or burial mound. Here is where, deep down, a three-thousand-year-old vase contains the mixed ashes of Achilles and Patroclus. Locals often report seeing a beautiful woman with black hair leaning against the mound.

Was it real? Or is it all a legend? All legends are based on a seed of truth. The stories had to come from something. So, yes, somewhere and at some time there really was a person who inspired someone to create Achilles. This inspirational person learned to live, to love, to grieve, and to die.

May we all be inspired by Achilles and find humanity within ourselves.

Made in the USA
Middletown, DE
14 January 2023